CLARKESV

D1197312

FICTION

NON-FICTION

Neil Clarke: Publisher/Editor-in-Chief
Sean Wallace: Editor
Kate Baker: Non-Fiction Editor/Podcast Director

Clarkesworld Magazine (ISSN: 1937-7843) • Issue 189 • June 2022

Company Town
AIMEE OGDEN

The company alarm sends Cass flailing out of bed with its first chime. If she lingers under the blankets, she'll disturb Maya: if she doesn't get up before the second alarm, the volume ratchets up to eighty decibels, and the smart thermostat will crank up the furnace to make the bedroom unpleasantly hot. She's not fully awake, though, until a blast of arctic air hits her in the face. Autopilot has carried her as far as the freezer; she gropes behind the ice maker until she finds the box of Veg-e-Saus; the last one. "Alexa, add veggie sausages to the shopping list. Oh, and run the dishwasher."

"Veggie sausages added," chirps Alexa, in her oh-so-punchable voice. "The dishwasher is offline."

A little yellow light blinks on the dishwasher control panel. NETWORK CONNECT ERROR, the readout insists. Without a connection, Cass can't run it, which means confronting the barricade of last night's dishes in the sink . . . later. For now, she opens the window over the sink to let some of the pleasant, dry morning air into the house. She and Maya are trying to save some Prime, right now, socking away a bit of savings. Running the AC below the company set point incurs a steep surcharge this time of year.

Four Veg-E-Saus clink onto a clean (albeit damp) plate; they slide around manically until Cass deposits them in the oven. Over the workaday buzz of microwave radiation, there's a squeak of cheap floorboards. Maya shuffles out of the bedroom and into the kitchen.

Somehow she's managed to get herself into her armor without making a sound: the intricate shoulder guards and breastplate, the winged helm. Cass takes a quick glance around, to make sure the curtains are all closed—yes, Maya's secret is safe for another morning.

1

Maya's sword hangs at her side, the purple crystal blade dark in its scabbard until her thumb strokes the hilt. A violet glow illuminates the kitchen and brusquely fades. No doubt there are places more deserving of its literally otherworldly illumination.

"I had the dream," she says guiltily. Guiltily but without an ounce of apology. "The Lord Revelator has raised an army of the undead, and—"

"You *just* got back from Modiru."

"You know time passes differently there. They need me." Maya breaks away from Cass' frown to buckle her sword-belt around her hips. "Hopefully I won't be gone long."

Long is an empty word, all meaning long since whittled away. Maya has been gone for minutes, and she's been gone for days. Once, she left during dinner and came home just as Cass was brushing her teeth for bed. Those two hours—just *two hours*—carved new scars into Maya's hands and arms and frosted her hair with gray. The gray faded overnight, while a restless Cass watched her sleep. The scars have stayed.

Cass opens the fridge and takes out the iced coffee, and then, just to have something to do, just to keep the door between her and Maya, she takes out an apple and the butter and the bag of English muffins and paws at the wall of yogurts like there's something she can't find. The work stoppage is in three days, and she can't say that out loud. Not just because the Alexa is on the counter, always listening—though yes, also, very much that. But also, she can't slap Maya in the face like that, right before she leaves. " . . . Hopefully not." At least they can talk about Modiru without triggering a keyword watchlist somewhere.

Gently, Maya closes the fridge, and Cass lets her. *I'll be back in time*, Maya doesn't say. *I know how much this matters.* When she leans in for a kiss, Cass tips her chin forward to meet her. Cass' lips are still gummy with sleep; they brush against Maya's and stick for a moment, without softening, before she brushes past. A sitcom-style peck, playacted without an audience. Or a laugh track, but there's nothing to smile about here. Cass slams the button to open the microwave. "I made sausage. Eat something before you go."

Maya fishes a Veg-E-Saus out of its greasy puddle and retreats toward the bedroom. "Thanks. I love you."

"Love you too." That, at least, feels real. Just not as real as an army of the undead, or a tenuous goblin-sprite alliance, or a magic word that can cut between realities. Cass hacks a chunk off one of the remaining Veg-E-Saus with her fork, turning her back on the flash of amethyst that pours through the bedroom door. The portal unravels as quickly as it formed, and Cass hasn't gotten any farther than salvaging the fake meat into a dozen tiny pieces by the time the shower turns on. She throws the whole plate in the sink to make a run for her five-minute hot water allowance.

Their house is on the outskirts of Assiduity—it's quieter out here, away from the company crèche and the grocery depot and the Smile District, of course, but more importantly, it's in the part of town with tiny yards and neck-high fences where nobody talks to their neighbors. It's more than they can really afford if they're trying to save up some Prime. But it means no one asks questions about Maya's comings and goings.

Cass used to ride her bike to work to save Prime, too, but someone broke the lock and took it off the porch last month. The neighborhood OrdeRing cams didn't capture any footage that they could use to identify the thief, and when Cass sent a complaint to the OrdeRing contact email, the autoresponder apologized and offered her fifteen percent off the price of any company-sold bike. Now some of their theoretical Prime savings are directed to a new bike fund.

In the meantime, she Loops in to work. The nearest station is two streets over; the Loop is just pulling up as Cass rounds the corner. She vaults over the residential delivery bots offloading from the Loop's undercarriage and boards just ahead of the closing doors. A soft ping lets her know that her fob has been successfully debited for the fare.

At the last stop before the Fresh District, a returning delivery drone jams in the Loop intake port. The interior lights turn off. "This Loop route is undergoing maintenance. Please disembark immediately."

Cass runs the rest of the way to Fresh and still crashes through the cafeteria's employee entrance six minutes late. "Sorry, sorry," she mutters as she ties on her apron and tucks her hair up inside her cap. The clock-in bot is immune to her apologies and gives her only three and a half stars for her start-of-shift eval: one deducted for tardiness, the other half for a smudge on her apron that didn't wash out.

Cass' station is between Liz and Paolo, who have already assembled and boxed a small stack of meals: Liz filling reheated and pre-prepped omelet patties, Paolo stacking breakfast sandwiches. Cass jerks a nod at them, and they respond in kind, not quite meeting her eye. They have every reason to be nervous—planning any kind of anti-company demonstration is a firing offense in the code of conduct—but this is ridiculous. If OrdeRing flags the interaction as suspicious enough to tag a manager, Cass has a lie locked and loaded. *Boss, I think someone in Fresh is tanking everyone else's ratings with one-bombs to try to hit the bestprepper bonus.* Maybe it's even true; Cass can pack a salad in thirty-four seconds, but she hasn't made bestprepper in three months.

And she starts in on salads right away, to get ahead of the lunch rush. Garden salads, first. Iceberg lettuce, shredded carrot, presliced egg, a single cross section of red onion, a plastic bag of croutons—all of it allocated into a biodegradable carton and sealed with one of Cass' workID stickers. It would be monotonous, if she didn't have to keep moving so fast. When her break alarm pings in her ear, she startles. She's been making salads for four hours without noticing the time go by—it's nice when that happens, when the rut ground down through the middle of her life widens enough to crush away boredom and doubt and sadness. It's awful when that happens, too. There's no time to think, and that's probably at least as much the point as "efficiency."

Paolo's break overlaps with hers by five minutes. When she's done gulping from her water bottle and fumbling in her bag for the River Bar she brought, he's waiting with a lopsided smile. "How's Maya?"

"Fine. Tired." Their official line is that Maya has a chronic illness. That fits with her remote work position (sometimes *very* remote) and most people aren't rude enough to ask for details. Lying to the company comes naturally to Cass but lying to friends grinds against her every instinct. Still, she keeps a mental spreadsheet of symptoms, medications, and prognoses to use against any sort of snoopiness emergency. "I don't think she's gonna be able to come out with us tonight, though."

"That sucks," says Paolo, but he leaves it at that. They eat their River Bars together in peace.

At ten, salads start deploying to customers. On her own lunch break, Cass calls up her prep ratings. Mostly fives, thankfully, but someone gave her a two because their hardboiled egg wasn't sliced all the way through.

Cass' eyes burn. A rating like that means someone is having a bad day, and that they decided the best way to deal with it was to make sure someone *else* had a bad day too. At her last job, before she took the bonus to move to Assiduity, she collected used cafeteria trays for the sanitizing station. She'd find wadded napkins, ketchup fingerpaint; sometimes people would smear honey on a tray and press a glass of ice water into it.

She's been off the bestprepper board all week anyway. It doesn't matter. It *shouldn't*, anyway. And soon, it won't. There are smarter people than her, organizing where the company can't see them. If the action spreads wide enough, if they can shut Assiduity down for three days, four, a week even, the losses will rack up. Eat shareholder value, motherfuckers.

4

The timer dings; Cass' lunch quarter is over. She puts away her phone and washes her hands and pulls out a bin of diced melon to start assembling afternoon snackpacks.

In the after-work dark, Cass goes out for a beer. Not to the Smile District, where there's a vice upcharge on all the booze, and all the bars are playing the same fifty most popular licensed music tracks. Instead, she jumps off the Loop on a residential street and turns up her coat collar to hide her face from the camera. At the door of an apartment building, she covers the Ring with her palm too, before buzzing to be let in. Through the doorstep, an aggressive bass line hammers the soles of her feet. No one asks her name before the door pops open to admit her. She slams it shut behind her to keep the screaming auralcore house music off the street.

Blackout curtains hang in each window, but the hallways are lit with pulsing electric blue and green. Some of the doorways stand open, revealing coolers heaped with melting ice and cans of out-of-company beer. Others invite entry, to join clusters of dancers. One is just far enough ajar for Cass to catch a glimpse of a man and woman: her face cramped in concentration where it presses against the wall; his bare ass clenching each time he thrusts. It's more privacy than the hallway, at least.

This party is a million code-of-conduct violations neatly boxed up in a single package: alcohol service outside the Smile District, distribution of non-company product, unpaid vice fees, unlicensed music, probably a banned substance or two on the higher floors. The company higher-ups have to be aware that this kind of thing goes on, but it's not worth their time to bother unless they get complaints. Maybe an angry neighbor will ping a supervisor, maybe not; if the party gets broken up, all the partygoers will have a fine taken off their Prime. OrdeRing might increase drone activity around the apartment complex, too. Everyone will complain, and it'll be hard to take the Prime hit, but that's the worst that'll happen.

That's why illicit activities are the best cover for other, *more* illicit activities.

Cass chooses a dance room at random, one that's pitch-black but for the glinting lights of the appliances. Her hips rub against someone's ass on one side, someone's dick on the other, before she presses past to take up space among the gyrating, sweaty bodies. The house music is loud, and the current track trips and skips out of the bootleg speakers, too fast for Cass' dizzy heartbeat to keep up. She dances anyway, swaying

5

her shoulders, thrusting her pelvis. Her entire body aches, knees and ankles and back, from a day at the prep table, but all that ebbs as she freefalls into the rhythm. She used to go out dancing more; she and Maya both. Now she only comes out if there's a good reason. She's going to feel it tomorrow, but that's Tomorrow Cass' problem.

Beneath the strobing purple lights, unfamiliar hands close on Cass' hips, and a warm body presses against her back. Even knowing what's coming, she tenses. "Noon," says a voice she doesn't recognize, right by her ear. Their two bodies sway in time. Sweat trickles between Cass' shoulder blades. "You're assigned to Gise Street depot. Warehouse ops break in the doors. Other divisions provide support, close ranks, and hold off K9 units while W-O's occupy the floor." Then they peel away, and Cass stumbles, losing the rhythm of the song.

She sticks around a little while after that, doing her part in turn: whispering *Gise Street depot* and *close ranks* and *occupy the floor* beneath curtains of hair and against stubbled cheeks. Three more days. Three more days. Flowery hair spray and grassy body spray fill her mouth when she breathes, and she sits in the hallway to crack a can of someone else's beer to wash away one artificial taste with another. A deep satisfaction rises upward from her belly, and it's definitely not from the beer. It felt good to move, cracking off the grime of the long workday. She misses Maya, watching her dance, eyes closed, the weight of two worlds forgotten for the spell of a song. Besides, loud music keeps people from asking the kinds of questions for which she and Cass might improvise mismatched answers.

Maybe after the strike, they'll go out again together. Cass presses into the wall with her back and shoves herself to her feet. Maybe after Maya comes home.

Cass waits up a while, after she stumbles into their house. Just in case. To pass the time, she browses shoe inserts on the company catalog—it makes her feel old as shit, but she's got what feels like plantar fasciitis in her left heel. Foot discomfort overrules emotional discomfort, in the end.

On a whim, she clicks the button to convert Prime to fiat currency: US dollars, Canadian, whatever she wants, or whatever she doesn't. The numbers feel impossibly heavy, outsized against the tiny pair of neon green gel pads. When the clock rolls around to 2:00 a.m., she gives up on shopping for now. After dry-swallowing two ibuprofen, she collapses in bed and kicks off all the covers.

She's on her feet in the kitchen before she realizes the alarm hasn't gone off yet. She takes her hand off the refrigerator door and squints at the flashing light where the automatic coffeepot is trying to remind her to fill it with beans and water. That light is out of sync with the one on the dishwasher, and for no good reason that annoys the absolute shit out of her. She gropes toward the cupboard where she keeps the coffee stuff and steps on a hand. *Maya's* hand.

"Maya!" She drops to her knees and cradles Maya's face. She can't look away from Maya's face because if she does, she'll have to look at all the blood everywhere else. "Maya, speak to me."

Maya's skin is warm and dry. Her eyelids flutter, then commit to opening. She focuses on Cass, one eye at a time, and smiles. "We did it," she croaks. A film of dried blood clings to her front teeth.

"You always do." Cass pulls off the hawk helm and casts it aside; she runs her fingers over Maya's armor. Cracks spiderweb outward from two clear impact points, but it seems to have held true. It's Maya's leg, bare beneath the gym shorts she likes to wear with her armor, where the real damage has been done. Linen bandages wrap her thigh; a broad, dark stain has spread between the layers. When Cass peels them back from the edge to peek at the damage, they stick to Maya's leg, and Maya's lips go pale and flat. "How long have you been lying here?"

"Don't know. Little while."

"You should have hollered! Why didn't you wake me up?"

Maya's glassy eyes take on a new shine. "You're always so *tired*, Cassie."

With some effort, and by closing off the part of her heart that clenches with every tight-lipped groan, Cass gets Maya off the floor and into the bathroom. Together, they manage to peel off the gym shorts and T-shirt and sports bra, and then it's into the tub, with three days' worth of hot water rations and a brand-new bar of soap. The alarm goes off while she's slowly peeling the crusted linen away from eight tiny stitches, done neatly, albeit with crude, fraying thread. Goblin handiwork, probably. They've got the tiny fingers for the job. And a knack for healing, which is why Maya usually fucking *stays* with them after a fight. Long enough to mend. Cass doesn't ask why she came back so quickly this time. Knowing hurts bad enough without having to hear Maya say it.

She leaves Maya to bathe while she goes to clean up. There's a big sticky brown spot on the kitchen tiles; she'll have to clean the grout later, with a toothbrush, when she has more time. Or maybe she won't. It's not like they're getting their security deposit back either way.

The unsheathed sword is on the floor, too, and there's a nick in the kitchen cabinet where the blade must have caught on its way down. Maybe they can fix that with some putty before they move out. Someday. She stoops to lift the sword. It's heavier than she expected, and when she holds it aloft, her shoulder burns.

Even as the hilt warms in her hand, the blade stays dark. Whatever secrets it holds, someone else was chosen to know them. Cass grunts and retrieves the sword belt from the cabinet it got kicked under. The scabbard swallows the murky blade, and Cass chucks the whole thing into the back of their closet. It can stay there, out of sight, until Maya needs it again. Until it needs *Maya* again.

When she comes back to the bathroom, Maya is still sitting, dripping, on the edge of the tub. Her hair is wet but still dirty, tumbling down her back half in and half out of its braid. "You're going to be late for work."

"I'm not fucking going to work today. I need to take you to Care! If this gets infected—"

"We have Neosporin in the medicine cabinet."

"What? How *old* is that? It's got to be expired. If you're not going to let a unicorn or whatever magic you healthy, then you need someone with a legit medical license to look at you."

"It'll cost Prime, and you need to go to work."

"Prime? Who fucking cares about our Prime? Do you think Prime matters more than—"

"They'll ask too many questions, Cassie!"

It's the reason she's been daring Maya to say out loud, and it still strikes her square in the chest. The tang of victory burns its way up her throat, and she sags against the bathroom counter. Maya's life and health and happiness matter more than Prime, but nothing is allowed to matter more than Modiru. " . . . I'm going to be late for work."

She throws on clothes, folds a piece of bread in half around a squirt of jelly, and crams her feet into her shoes. When she opens the front door, she pauses a second. The floorboards creak, but Maya doesn't say anything. Doesn't ask her to stay.

Cass lets the door bang shut behind her.

Before her first break of the morning, Cass has sent out five salads without tomato and used the wrong cheese on another half dozen. Instead of choking down the snackpack she bought with her employee discount, she spends her fifteen minutes crying in a bathroom stall— except she actually spends eighteen minutes, not fifteen, and gets docked the full half-hour of work time.

"How's Maya?" whispers Liz when Cass finally returns and puts on a fresh pair of prep table gloves.

Apparently Cass' efforts to hide her wound-red eyes behind her bangs have been wasted. "Oh, fine," she says, too brightly. "Pretty tired, but when is she *not*, you know?"

8

Liz and Paolo exchange a glance. Cass counts olives: one, two, three, four, and into the box, press and seal, label, load it into the dispenser, and kiss it goodbye. She texts Maya twice during the day. At ten, she sends: *Text back if you're alive please* and receives a thumbs-up emoji in answer. After lunch, she tries again. *Let me know if there's anything you need me to pick up on the way home.* That one gets a Read receipt, but no response.

By the time Cass Loops home, she's encased herself in a bright, brittle shell of Normalcy. When she unlocks the front door, Maya is lying on the couch that serves as their living room and dining table. Her eyelids twitch at the sound of the key, but she doesn't look over.

"I brought leftover sandwiches from work," Cass says in the most casual voice she can muster. She gets an extra fifteen percent discount on unsold food, although she's not allowed to buy the ones she packaged herself. "Do you want chicken salad with barbecue chips or ham and Swiss, also with barbecue chips?"

Maya doesn't open her eyes. "Cass."

The weight of her own name is all it takes to crack through her protective armor. Her nose starts running first, then her throat closes around its sudden soreness. She drops the sandwich containers on the counter and slams the bathroom door behind her. On the toilet, hunched over, she chokes on the sobs that claw their way out of her and soaks half a roll of toilet paper. When the tears find their way into her mouth, they taste like old makeup and salt and something hateful—something that needed to be excreted and thrown away.

What returns to her, slowly, isn't calm, but it's a good enough substitute. It's composure, at least; makeshift, but functional. She uncurls from the toilet lid and splashes cold water on her face at the sink. She opens the door and leans into the doorknob, unable to walk out into the kitchen yet. " . . . Sorry. I'm sorry. For—"

It's the *for* that catches her up and sets her eyes burning again. She's not sorry for hating Modiru. She's not sorry for wishing that portal would never open and rip Maya through it again. She treasures all that not-sorry up and holds it close. "I'm sorry for not being strong enough for you."

"That's not . . . " Maya pushes up on her elbows. "Do you think that's what bothers me? That I think you're *weak*?"

They stare at each other until Maya breaks first and lowers herself back down. "I'm sorry too," she says. "That I let you think that."

She has her own things that she's not sorry for, of course, and just like Cass, she keeps those for herself alone. But she slides her legs off the couch, carefully, moving slow, and Cass, carefully, moving slow, sits in the warm space beside her. She puts one arm around Maya's shoulders, and Maya crushes herself against her. All the things they're not sorry for remain, but not between them; they've left no space for that.

Hunger finally pulls them apart. Maya opts for the chicken salad and rolls up her pajama pant-leg to inspect her wound while Cass heaves herself to a stand. "I think it's looking better. Less puffy and red. I still heal fast, even without unicorn intervention. One of the benefits of the job."

"At least one of us has tangible job benefits." Cass dumps the sandwiches from the cartons onto actual plates (that she'll have to handwash later, but whatever, it feels somehow both normal and special to not eat off cardboard).

"Do you . . . want to talk about it?"

"Will it upset you?"

"I'm a big girl." Which means *yes, but do it anyway.*

They've been together long enough that Maya speaks Cass' language. In between bites, she recounts a battle. To her, the story is epic; to Cass, who's no kind of hero, it's terrifying: the arrival of the wolf-men of Baros, newly allied to the Lord Revelator's cause. Goblin forces pinned between the undead and the slavering jaws of the wolf-men. A feint from General Blightwind's wyverns, barely repelled, and the undead army rallying to finish the job—Maya pauses to wipe barbecue chip crumbles off her sweatshirt—until the centaurs and sprites, united beneath Prince Theodalus' banner, rode into battle and shattered the Lord Revelator's forces under their spears.

As the battle winds down, Maya pauses, examining her orange-tinted fingertips. " . . . Do *you* want to talk about—it?"

Cass glances sidelong at the Alexa on the kitchen counter. Talking about *it* would relieve some of the pressure in her chest; talking about *it* might also ensure that *it* doesn't happen. "Forward progress," she says, generically. "Things are moving along. You know."

Maya nods. She has carried encrypted codes behind enemy lines, and she knows Cass' keywords by heart. "Sure," she says. She touches Cass' cheek, and for the first time Cass sees the mirror-image of her own fear, each time she watches Maya step through that portal. "Good. Well. Be careful. Okay?"

"Okay," she whispers, but what does she have to be careful about? She's not Maya, leading armies into battle. She's not an organizer, risking safety and stability and freedom to give hope to thousands of others. She's Cass. All she does is make salads and wait for someone else to tell her what to do.

They have just two days to fall into the rut of routine. Gears clicking together, a clockwork set of motions to move them through their schedule. Wake, eat, work, eat, rest. Cass has gotten pretty fucking good at not thinking too much, considering that's how she spends ten hours a day at her prep table six times a week. The comfort of routine liberates her from having to think too much about any of it: about the unnatural speed with which Maya's wounds heal, about the fights they've had, and the ones they refuse to. About the work stoppage. About being the girlfriend that is *worried about* and not the girlfriend that *worries*.

It's only in the dark of the night that she has too much time and too much quiet to keep the thoughts of her head. She's had to come to grips time and again with the fact that she's not the only one who's chosen Maya, and that one of these days, she might lose her to that other. Maya's just now having the thought that she might lose *Cass* first.

"Maya," she says, in the 2:00 a.m. dark. It's the night before the work stoppage, and her lips move against Maya's cool, salt-smelling neck. "I . . . " She can't get any farther past a pang of guilt.

But Maya isn't asleep. She rolls toward Cass and fumbles her hand inside Cass' shirt. Her palm slides up Cass' ribs, and Cass pushes up onto her elbow to find Maya's mouths with her own. Their lips cling together as Maya slides her good leg between Cass'. It's too dark to see, but Cass stares down into the space where Maya is, as if she could see her, if she just tried hard enough. If she just wanted it badly enough.

She wakes up with a start, her hand still in Maya's boxers, and fumbles her feet onto the floor. She's groping for the kitchen light switch when she realizes that what's woken her isn't the morning alarm; it's the town alert system blasting at top volume from the Alexa . . . and outside the windows as well.

"—to remain in your houses today," a robotic corporate voice announces, with a discordant calm. "Do not leave for work, food, or recreation. Anyone discovered breaking curfew, whether employee, guest, minor, or other uncategorized resident, will be taken into custody. This curfew will be in effect from dawn on April 15 until dawn on April 16. All residents of Assiduity are directed to remain in your houses today. Do not leave—"

"Fuck!" Cass cracks the front door to peer out. A pair of K9s patrol the street, their unpleasantly angled robot legs tip-tapping at a jaunty pace. Their glassy eyes swivel left and right, searching. "Fuck fucking *fuck.*"

All the care they've taken, all the steps to avoid the company's notice, and management still got tipped off. Someone must have squealed, probably hoping for a big fat financial pat on the head from their higher-ups. If Cass ever finds out who—and she knows she won't, but *if*—she'll kick their ass so hard that future astronauts will discover frozen rectal fragments on the fucking moon.

Or maybe there wasn't a rat at all. It's not like she's ever met an organizer, face-to-face. That's the whole point of the system they've devised, after all. Maybe this was a company op from the start: plan a fake strike, kneecap it before it even starts. Cost all the employees in the city a day's Prime and make them question how much it's really worth it, to cause this kind of trouble.

A shuffle of footsteps behind her. It's Maya, eyes wide and wild, sporting an epic case of bedhead. "Fuck," Cass repeats. "I didn't mean to shout. They know about the *thing*, babe." *The thing.* Christ. Even now, instinct keeps her from naming it aloud.

Another, deeper instinct unfurls too, and her breath catches. She can see the marks of tears on Maya's face. "No. *No.* Don't say it—"

Maya pulls her flannel (Cass' flannel) higher up on her shoulder. "I had the dream," she says quietly and meets Cass' eyes.

Of course she did. Of course. But there's no anger left in Cass; that's been purged, or sublimated, last night, into an ache deep enough to scar. She sinks to the arm of the couch; not because she planned to sit there, just because she found it before she found the floor.

"Why do you always have to go that way?" she asks. Not angrily; there's anger there, down inside her, but she can't quite reach it now. It feels like someone else's. Maybe it always has been. "How come, I don't know, there's never a centaur princess wizard popping over here to shoot arrows into the board of directors' eyeholes? Why can't *you* stay? I know not every problem can be solved with a sword, but . . . "

"But some can. Yeah." Maya walks across the room and grasps Cass' face, her fingernails digging in against the back of Cass' neck. Her lips are cool on Cass' forehead. "You're *my* hero. I hope you know that."

Cass doesn't know anything. She nods dully, which breaks the seal of Maya's kiss. Maya lets go of her reluctantly and returns to the bedroom. The clatter of armor is a familiar prelude to the electric thrum of the portal—the violet light flashes, then folds in on itself, leaving white aftershocks on Cass' vision.

She stays on the couch until the color comes back to her sight. Being in pajamas still, at this time, goes against the expectations ingrained in her. She shuffles toward the bedroom and stops.

Maya is gone. The sword is not.

Abandoned, but not forgotten. She picks it up from the bed, belt and all. It's still heavy, even sleeping in its scabbard. When she draws it, the blade stays dull and dark, but the hilt feels solid in her hand. When Cass turns the blade, testing its weight, it shows her a glimmer. She almost drops it—but that's just the dishwasher light and the coffeepot, blinking close enough together that it seems tandem. As long as she doesn't watch too long, waiting.

She peeks between the kitchen curtains. In the other houses, her neighbors' faces make vague pink-and-brown murals. Some of them surely expected to be at Gise Street today at noon, or one of the other depots, or standing on Loop lines, or downing delivery drones. Everyone's watching. No one knows what to do.

Cass sure as hell doesn't. And she doesn't know if anyone else is going to follow her if she walks outside. She doesn't know if a sword this size could take the head off a K9 or bust down a depot door. She doesn't even know what all this is *for*, anymore. If she walks out that door and starts turning OrdeRing drones into scrap heaps and someone said *hey, knock it off*, doesn't she need a list of demands in hand to say, *sure, I'll stop, but first, you've gotta—*?

She knows very little. But she knows how to buckle a belt, even a sword belt, and she knows to jam her feet into shoes before she steps outside. As the K9 heads turn her way, she knows to adjust her grip on the hilt of the sword, getting a feel for its weight. It seems to know, too, its own purpose, and it doesn't fight her as she brings it to bear.

Faces move behind the windows. Voices spill into the yards. She doesn't know how many will join her, but she knows some of them will. The dominoes are trembling, but for now, they remain standing. No one wants to be the first to fall. But someone's going to be.

Maybe it'll be Cass. She steps back into a guard stance, and a shimmer of sunlight travels the length of the blade. Maybe. But not yet.

The first K9 charges, gearing up for a takedown; two more hang back, at its sides, to deploy subdual measures. Cass bares her teeth and steps into her swing like some kind of crazed medieval Babe Ruth.

Of all the things she knows, the truest is this: she is already one person's hero. And she thinks, maybe, she could be her own, too.

ABOUT THE AUTHOR

Aimee Ogden is a former software tester and science teacher; now she writes stories about sad astronauts and space mermaids. Her debut novella "Sun-

Daughters, Sea-Daughters" is a 2021 Nebula finalist, and her short fiction has appeared in publications such as *Lightspeed, Analog,* and *Beneath Ceaseless Skies,* as well as previously in *Clarkesworld.* She also co-edits *Translunar Travelers Lounge,* a magazine of fun and optimistic speculative fiction.

The Art of Navigating an Affair in a Time Rift

NIKA MURPHY

In this timeline, crayons litter the kitchen table. Red for Mars. Pink and orange for clouds. Cerulean for the dot in the sky I call home, in this timeline. Jeannie sticks out her tongue when she colors. Her knuckles turn white as she rubs the crayons to nubs. She hands the picture to me as flakes of wax fall to the floor like confetti.

"It's beautiful, Jeannie," I say and kiss her forehead. She smells like earth after the rain. I hang it next to the others on the fridge. Her drawings overlap my sketches. Two artists in the family, as my husband likes to say. Jeannie runs outside to play. I tiptoe to the front of the house and push the blinds back an inch.

Joseph, the man who moved in across the street last year, dug a koi fishpond in his front yard and planted bamboo ten meters high. The lady on the corner crocheted him a stuffed panda that hangs from one of the trees. In some timelines, the panda is a dragon. In one timeline, the dragon has eaten all the koi. In that agonizing timeline, Joseph does not want me at all.

In most timelines, though, I borrow Joseph's comic books. He borrows my postapocalyptic paperbacks. We talk about robots and Bradbury and art. He's out there now. Shirtless. Feeding the fish. Their mouths breach the water in hungry little O's.

My husband pulls into the driveway, blocking my view with the Jeep. He gives me a kiss when he walks in and asks about Jeannie.

"She's out back," I say.

"You've got Outlier testing in an hour, Audra. You said you'd get her ready," Paul says, his Texas drawl more prominent when he loses his patience.

"Sorry, I lost track of time," I say.

Paul smiles, and his dimples melt away my thoughts. When I married him right out of high school, I never expected him to amount to anything. I always underestimated him, even before the rift sent us all into parallel timelines, before me and other Outliers pinballed in and out of pocket universes while the rest shifted into cozy sister dimensions. When he made Varsity or when the Space Force promoted him. I thought, at some point, he'd fail, and I'd no longer have to justify why we were together.

"It's okay," he says and gathers up the crayons. His perfection stands so tall, it towers over me and leaves me in shadow.

My nose tickles as if I'm about to sneeze, and I shift into another dimension. Not all transitions through the rift are gentle. Gentle means life will be more or less normal here.

In this timeline, Jeannie is at school and Paul is at the Institute. The phone buzzes. It's Joseph. My entire body burns when I see his name on the screen. My insides curdle and petrify. My heart beats against my chest like a moth against a lamp. I shiver and answer the call.

"Come over," he says in a voice like snow on the sidewalk. Soft, sibilant, gray. He knows I am alone. I press the phone to my ear and soak in his sound waves.

I grab some books and the comics I borrowed and walk across the street. He leaves the door open for me. Johnny Cash's voice crackles from the stereo. He sings "I'm on Fire."

"That's how I feel when I know you are close," Joseph says. I don't respond. He takes my books and comics. Incense burns in the window and fills the house with a blurry haze. I want to drown in this smell.

"Do you have something new for me?"

"Try this," he says and hands me Superman with a Soviet hammer and sickle on his chest. When I try to take it, he doesn't let go. "For your thoughts."

"How about a penny instead?"

"How about a dance?"

Joseph tosses the comic on a chair. Its pages flip open and flutter. I want to dance, but I ask for a rain check instead.

He stands and watches me and sighs.

Hours slip by like brushstrokes. We talk about new shows and old films. We sit on the floor and flip through art books. We study each other. I memorize the wrinkles around his eyes. The shape of his lips. The scar on his eyebrow. We try not to touch. But the tips of my fingers meet his, and his skin electrifies me. Skin like packed powder. Like it could crumble and blow away if we give in and embrace.

The rift scratches at my periphery. Smudges the edges of my mind with dry bristles.

"I have to go," I say, but I don't move.

The rift takes me anyway.

Paul and Jeannie walk in front of me down the Institute halls. Boys and girls in lab coats who can't possibly be old enough to study or work here walk past. I wonder if I looked like that before I graduated college.

Paul is explaining how the machine stimulates your neurons to realign your consciousness to your "dimension of origin." He may as well be speaking Japanese. I majored in Art History. In some timelines, I am the one explaining the rift to Jeannie while Paul stares blankly at the back of my head.

Dr. Kuzbari greets us with clipboard in hand and escorts us to the Neurotemporal Alignment Lab. We go over the standard questions, and I wait for Paul and Jeannie to finish their sessions.

"Your turn, Mrs. Cobb," she says even though I tell her to call me Audra. I shoot a glance back to Paul.

"You'll do great," Paul smiles and gives me two thumbs up.

Dr. Kuzbari waits for me to sit in the leather chair before elevating it. She gives me the feedback helmet and lets me put it on myself. Then she clicks it into the humming machine behind me and checks the sensors for what seems like an hour.

I hate this room. The ecru walls suffocate me. The lights dim and monitors flicker and beep like a techno music video. The helmet's headphones squeeze my ears, and they begin to ache. I try to readjust in the recliner, but it squeaks and snaps and I worry I broke it.

"Just relax," the doctor says. She positions the visor over my eyes. "Almost ready," she says in her lilting accent as she types nonstop.

"How long have you been doing this?" I say.

"Thirty years now. I was a neuropsychiatrist in my old timeline."

"You seem so young." I shift my weight but find no comfort.

"Thank you," she says, and the typing finally stops. "You may feel some discomfort when the helmet activates the rift. This is normal."

The visor flashes green dots, and I feel like I've been yanked inside out. I brace myself for what comes next.

The shift is violent, and I pray my time in this place will be swift. The noises and lights disappear and leave me in a void. It's not black or white, but colorless, like the back of my eyelids. Then walls appear one by one. My walls. My house. I walk to the window and watch for Joseph to appear. He steps out on the porch and waves at me. I wave back.

Thank gods. There are timelines where Joseph does not exist. Timelines where I am a lizard in a terrarium in my own house watching on as my husband makes love to another wife. Where my child is but stardust. Living through those rifts, however momentary, feels like being pressed through a sieve.

Suddenly, the house starts to shake. The floor pulsates, shelves spit out books, and paintings jump from the walls like crickets. I try to hang on. I bang my fist against the window, but Joseph only waves.

The vibrations thump and the windows explode. Glass snows on my hair and bounces on the rug. The house levitates. I reach through the broken window and cut my hand on a shard of glass. The blood flows down my arm, down the stucco, and evaporates in the fireball of rocket boosters below. My house transforms into a rocket amid liftoff. I lean out of the window and call for help, but Joseph only waves.

Joseph waves goodbye.

I scream, but my voice dissolves in the roar of the flames. I sob, but the wind dries my face.

When the boosters sputter through the last layers of the atmosphere and the house is quiet again, I wade through the floating rubble to the kitchen. Curtains billow in a zero-gravity breeze, but my feet stick to the floor. Jeannie plucks crayons from the air and draws three-dimensional crystal domes. Paul takes me in his arms and grooms glass chunks out of my hair. He kisses my forehead, and I nestle into the nook between his shoulder and his heart.

Guilt overwhelms me, and I pull away. I run to the open window and jump.

Dr. Kuzbari switches the visor and headphones off. My eyes burn as they adjust to the light in the room, in a foreign timeline. My joints ache in the Martian gravity.

I sigh.

I hate Mars.

"What did the doc say?" Paul asks on the ride home. The weak Martian sun sets behind the passing trees in an autumnal blur. A Mango Tango crayon rolls across the floor mat.

"She wants to run some tests. She thinks I'm manipulating the machine, well, not me, my brain. She thinks my brain is controlling the shifts."

"You're in good hands with her. She's the leading expert in the field. Anyway, it won't be much longer. They're days away from calculating a solution to the rift. We could go home soon. To our own timeline."

Home. I stare out the window at Phobos and Deimos. Pimples in the burned Martian sky.

"Remember when we lived on Earth?"

Paul intertwines our fingers and kisses my hand. The sight of his profile untangles my thoughts.

"In another timeline?" he asks.

"You don't remember?"

"It's enough to know we were all together."

"I'm hungry," Jeannie yells from the backseat. We pick up a pizza and Jeannie recites all the new words she learned in school. We giggle when she mispronounces terra*foam* and Valla *Marinara*. In every timeline, their laughter eclipses all my resentments until they shrink to asteroids crashing into the sun.

A few days later, I'm back at the Institute for another session. Beige walls close in on me. Dr. Kuzbari straps me to a gyroscopic chair. It's supposed to help with the nausea. Instead, I feel like an actor stuck on the set of a foreign horror movie.

Lights, camera, shift, the sensation of being sucked through a straw.

This seems familiar. I've seen this in another timeline. My house. Again, we take off into the sky. Again, the agony of Joseph's goodbye. Then Jeannie and her domes. Paul and his love. I run to the window, swat the debris away like gnats, and jump through. But the transition doesn't save me.

I fall and fall toward Earth, all blue and brown and cotton candy wrapped. Her gravity pulls me closer. The wind and cold penetrate my bones.

"Audra," Earth whispers. My name echoes on her breath and draws me in. I close my eyes and let her jet streams carry me.

Paul catches me in mid-flight and jerks me upward. He wears a Superman cape. The symbol on his chest shines brighter than the sun. When I squint, a picture of our family emerges. I beg him not to take me back, but he pumps one fist in the air and heads toward the red dot in the sky while I struggle to break free.

I am still screaming when Dr. Kuzbari removes my visor, and the rift spits me back into the lab. She loosens my restraints, brings me a glass of water, and waits for me to calm down, for my heart rate to slow, for my breathing to steady. Then she speaks.

"You want to tell me what is happening with you?"

"I don't know."

"You can tell me. Whatever it is."

"I don't want to go home," I blurt out. She leans forward in her chair.

"A common sentiment among Outliers," she says. "Tell me, can you control your jumps?"

"Is that possible?"

"Is it?" She leans back, disappointment oozing from her tone. She pauses, hesitant to say whatever itches at her.

"Tell me about the man. The neighbor," she says at last.

The words don't form. I gather my things.

"If you find me, the old me, here at the Institute, will you talk to me? To her?"

"The neuropsychiatrist?" I think on it but leave without answering.

Once outside, I run and keep running. I can be home in fifteen minutes if I keep going, so I do. I run and run all the way to my street, and I collapse at Joseph's door. I knock, but he doesn't answer. I call but he doesn't pick up. I sit back against his door and cry. The rift squeezes my lungs, and I shift again.

The koi fish play and chase each other until they swirl into a ribbon of color cutting through the pond. The ribbon coils around the bamboo trees and shoots into the sky like a drunken rainbow.

Tears drip down my face, then hopscotch into the pond. Even if I could control the damned rift, what would I do? I can't split myself in half and live in familial bliss with Paul and Jeannie while my quantum twin dives into Joseph's bed and never again comes up for air. The two Audras would obliterate each other and create a black hole that swallows the entire universe.

Paul pulls up and helps Jeannie out of the car. He shoos her inside before I can say hi.

"What the heck is going on?" he asks, his accent thick and cartoonish.

"I don't know," I say.

"You scared me half to death. Doctor Kuzbari said you shouldn't be left alone."

I don't disagree.

Paul talks but I have trouble listening. I hear him say words like "adverse effects" and "gravitational collapse," but all I can focus on is Joseph's door.

"Audra, are you listening to me?" Paul snaps his fingers, and I look into his blue-gray eyes. I want to smooth the worry in his brow. To make our lives perfect again. He hugs me the way he does in my favorite timelines, and I don't pull away until he does.

• • •

It's wrong, but sometimes I imagine Joseph when Paul makes love to me. I don't open my eyes until we are done. Afterward, I feel so guilty, I shower for forty-five minutes. But not in Martian timelines. On Mars, we use synthetic towels to scrub our skin to conserve water. You can get used to any timeline, Paul says. Nothing ever bothers him.

On Earth, wisps of steam trail behind me as I step out of the bathroom. They follow me into the bedroom.

"You are so beautiful," Paul says. I crawl back into bed and fall asleep in the crook of his arm.

A knock on the bedroom door wakes me deep in the night.

"Mommy." Jeannie whimpers from behind the locked door.

"I'll get it." Paul starts to get up.

"No, it's my turn," I say.

"Let me. You need your rest."

I'm already up, bathrobe on. "Next time."

The dim light of the hallway forms long shadows on the hardwood, on the walls, on the ceiling. I pick Jeannie up and tell her that skinny giants are following us on the way to her room. They writhe and shrivel into the corners. Jeannie giggles and nuzzles her head in my neck. Her eyelashes tickle my skin, and her tears soak through my nightgown.

"I had a bad dream," she mumbles.

"Me too," I say and stroke her hair, rubbing the tangles between my fingers. I tuck her in and lie next to her. The shadows snake along the edges of the room.

"What did you dream, Mommy?"

"I dreamed we lived on Mars, but it was too hot, and we all dried out and turned into dust."

"That's silly. It's always cold on Mars because the sun is too far away," Jeannie says. "The *virgin* sucks out all the heat."

I hold back laughter. Shadows bobble and grin and drip from the windowsills and light fixtures. "Virga," I correct her.

"I think the Virga is beautiful," she says and wiggles her tiny fingers to make pretend rain fall from the pretend sky.

I wiggle my fingers with her, and the rift opens like a book. My muscles tense against its pull but relax when Jeannie snuggles against me. Her love is gravity and tethers me to her, to this timeline. Clouds form beneath the glow-in-the-dark stars on the ceiling. The temperature in the room drops to freezing. Our breath puffs out of our nostrils and mouths like steampunk robots. Brilliant snowflakes fall from the clouds but dissipate before touching us. "Virga," I whisper.

We watch the snow twinkle for a while until the rift closes, and we both fall asleep.

Smells of bacon and coffee climb the stairs and wake me. I follow the scent to the kitchen and join Paul and Jeannie for family breakfast. We look like a cereal commercial.

Except the scene is all askew. The walls tilt and the floorboards pulsate.

"How do you want your eggs?" Paul asks.

"Over easy," I say. But before the words leave my mouth, the steaming plate appears in front of me. I break the yolk with my fork, and it oozes and swirls onto the table and onto the floor and sparkles as it winds its way through the dining room to the living room and up the stairs. I want to follow it, but Paul stops me.

"Where are you going? Aren't we going to talk about the R-I-F-T?"

"Daddy, I know how to spell rift," Jeannie says and pouts at us.

"The Institute has found a way to close it," he says. "We can finally go back."

Go back.

The words echo and reverberate through the house. The egg yolk path glistens in my periphery and my fingertips tingle. Once the rift closes, we go back. Back to before the rift ruptured. Back to when Joseph first moved in and before we . . .

Before.

I have to tell Joseph.

I excuse myself and follow the shining egg yolk toward the door. It loops around and goes up the stairs, but I ignore it and stumble out into the front yard. I look up and down the street, and I know I am looking for something. For a pond. But it's not there. Paul comes outside and takes my hand.

"What are you looking for, Audra?"

"I think, a house. Wasn't there a house right there?" I ask and point across the street to the slide and swings and monkey bars sprouting like time lapse weeds from the empty spot where Joseph's house stood yesterday.

"You forgot again, didn't you?" Paul says and smiles. The kind of smile I give Jeannie when she mixes up her left and right shoes.

"I'm sorry," I say. Maybe Joseph was always part of the rift. Maybe it's better this way and eventually I will forget he ever existed. Forget I ever wanted to tear my heart out and let him devour it.

"It's always been this way, baby," Paul says and hugs me and walks me back into the house.

Isn't this what I wanted? Without Joseph, everything fits. Everything makes sense. My life. My family. My place in the world. I am a good wife in this timeline. A good mother. I smile.

"It's perfect," I lie.

The kitchen is still sideways. And the egg yolk path still beckons me upstairs.

The Laser Lemon yolk breathes and whispers as it meanders up each step. I follow its glimmering trail until I reach Jeannie's bedroom door. A blinding white light flashes through the cracks. I put my hand on the knob, but I don't turn it.

If I turn the knob, this world will melt away. If I turn around, I can stay here. Jeannie and Paul call my name from behind the door. They yell, scream, "Audra!" "Mommy!"

I turn the knob and walk through the barrier of light, but Paul and Jeannie aren't there. I am. I am asleep in Jeannie's bed. I run over to my sleeping self and shake her.

"Wake up, Audra," I say.

She opens her eyes, and we collide into another timeline together.

Dr. Kuzbari's neuropsychiatric office is small and dark. A sliver of window. A yellowing vine on the sill. Dust caresses the overflowing bookshelves. The room smells of oiled brass and turmeric. She walks in with two mugs and hands me one, then sits with the cup in front of her as the steam obscures her face.

"Are you ready to tell me about the man?"

I breathe in the spiced tea and take a sip. It burns my tongue.

"He's my neighbor. We haven't . . . We haven't done anything."

"It's an emotional affair?"

"It's not love," I clarify.

"Lust then? That's certainly simpler."

"No." I blow on my tea to cool it. "It's like a worm that has burrowed its way into my stomach and claws and bites me until I feed it moments with him."

"Limerence," she says. "Not so simple after all."

We sit in silence and sip our teas for a minute.

"In my timeline, you're a famous neurophysicist. You'll close the rift."

She smirks as her eyes search the distance. I wonder which timeline she would prefer if given the choice. Her face turns solemn. She leans forward. Pushes her mug aside. "You can have him," she says.

"What do you mean?"

"You can have the man, the neighbor, in this timeline and every other, if that is what you want."

"But?"

"No but. You can choose him."

"But I'll lose my family."

"Yes."

No.

A frayed thread tickles my neck like Jeannie's lashes. I tug and the rift unravels.

I jump through razor wire to another dimension.

Smells of bacon and coffee climb the stairs and wake me. I follow the scent to the kitchen and join Paul and Jeannie for family breakfast.

"How do you want your eggs?" Paul asks.

"Over easy," I say. "No, wait." This is all wrong. "Don't we need to talk about L-O-V-E?"

Jeannie pouts at me.

"What about?" Paul says.

Something is stuck in my throat, and I can't respond. I get up from the table and run out the front door across the street to Joseph's. I knock and ring the bell and knock again, and he answers, but I can't breathe, and I can't tell him what I think because my mind is all pictures and colors and the light from outside is so very bright that I can't see.

"What's wrong, Audra? Tell me. Please tell me," Joseph says with his hands around my shoulders, searching with his eyes, and it's his face when he makes love to me in my imagination.

"I want to stay with you, but I can't," I say and collapse into his arms, and I sob as he cradles me back and forth and runs his fingers through my hair.

"Stay with me," he says. "Stay."

"I can't. I'm sorry."

"Please don't go."

"Goodbye."

I walk back to my house and lock myself in the upstairs bathroom. I run hot water in the bath and the sink until steam covers the mirror, and I can no longer see my reflection.

I must find a way to be with Joseph and with Paul and with Jeannie. Surely, there are dimensions where I have unbounded wealth, fame, superpowers. Dimensions where I can destroy worlds or build them. Where I can live forever. If I can just focus and keep the rift open long enough, I can find a way to keep them all.

Paul knocks on the door.

"Talk to me, Audra," he says. His voice is distorted, so I turn off the faucets to hear him better, but I don't unlock the door.

"I don't know what to say." Water droplets snake down the mirror and plop into the standing water. "I don't know what to do."

"Sure you do. Let me in, baby."

The faucets drip. It sounds like the world after rain.

"I just need a little more time."

"The man across the street." There's pain and hesitation in his voice. "Are you . . . ?"

"No, never," I say. "In any of the timelines, I swear."

"Because I would understand. He's more like you. I mean, you know what I mean. I'm not. I'm not like that. But I know you. I know you love your family. I love you so much, Audra. I've loved you since I was fourteen years old. You're the only woman I ever loved, and I don't know how to save us, but I'll find a way."

"You don't need to save us, Paul. You're not Superman."

"I know. I know. Will you let me in?"

"Go away, please. I want to be alone."

"Okay. I'll be here whenever you're ready to come out. I'll always be here for you."

I wait until his footsteps fade away. I peek under the door to check, and see Jeannie's eye staring back at me.

"Mommy, are you okay?"

"Yes, baby, I'm taking a bath."

"No, you're not. I can see your feet."

I smile.

"I made you a picture." She slides it under the door.

Me, Paul, and Jeannie in front of our house. She's starting to grasp perspective and shadow. Much better than I did at her age.

I cry and let the tears of pride, of shame, evaporate in the steam as my heart squeezes out its last shard of resistance.

The rift pulses in my ears and opens doors to lives where Joseph and I dance in orbit around each other. Cold lives where nothing shines except when we are together. And even then, the heat we generate is tepid. Like putting a hand in the fireplace and finding fake fire, plastic wood, glass embers. Lives where I am never truly satisfied. Not without Paul and Jeannie.

Without them, I'm a shell made up of sketches and vinyl records and yellowed pages. Without them, I am empty.

It's impossible. There is no dimension or timeline before or after the rift where I get to have them all. But there are an infinity of timelines where Paul loves me, where Jeannie came from my body and inherited my love of art. Where I am loved whole, shell and brain and sinew. None of those timelines include Joseph.

I step into the tub and submerge myself. The water washes away the murk swirling in my brain and the rift shines white like a blank canvas. I breathe out and the air bubbles paint a door. I step through.

Dr. Kuzbari operates the rift machine. Paul stands off to the side, but I know he is there. I know he will see everything on the monitors.

"See you at home, Mommy," Jeannie says.

The straps around my waist and my wrists are loose. Kuzbari's got me hooked to an oxygen mask and an IV and a host of machines. A thousand electrodes protrude from my head.

"Alright, Mrs. Cobb, we are ready, how about you?" says the doc, resting the visor on my forehead.

"Blast off," I say.

"Godspeed," she whispers in Earth's voice.

I close my eyes and let the beige walls fall away one last time.

My street stretches in a slight curve to the west. The sun sets behind a group of mismatched houses and trees, old and tall. Spanish moss hangs in thick curtains from the branches. The sky is all the colors of Jupiter at once soaked in summer air.

Joseph stands at the edge of his koi pond. I want to go to him. To lose myself for hours in comics and music and carelessness. To yearn and drown in the yearning, suspended in the margin between despair and wild abandon, a space where happiness always lies beyond the horizon. But the waning light from the sun shines on my house and leaves Joseph's in the dark. So, I go home.

As I step inside, the rift closes behind me and melts away.

Colored pencils roll across the kitchen table. Jeannie's tongue sticks out as she adds sunglasses to the yellow sun.

"That's clever, Jeannie." I breathe in her scent as I kiss the top of her head. She smells of home.

Paul comes in and kisses me.

"Did you see our new neighbor is diggin' a pond?" Paul shakes his head. "Imagine the mosquitoes!"

"Can we get pizza for dinner?" Jeannie asks.

Something catches in my throat, but it's gone in a blink along with trillions of memories.

ABOUT THE AUTHOR

Nika Murphy is a Ukrainian-born writer of speculative fiction. When she's not busy working on her fiction MFA at Arcadia University, she subsidizes her typewriter collection with a day job in the pharmaceutical industry. She resides in Florida with her family.

Manjar dos Deuses
ANNA MARTINO

I.

"Some would say it's mercenary to charge people for their memories. What do you have to say about that?"

Trust a reporter to sour the beauty of my work, Daniel thought. "I'm not charging for their memories. I'm charging for the reconstruction. Every one of my clients is special—every food memory is unique, and it's my job to treat it like the treasure it is. This is not an easy feat but, as you have just testified, it's money well spent."

The reporter laughed in embarrassed agreement as she nibbled on another prawn from the cocktail Daniel prepared according to her dearest memory, her first "grown up" event: a wedding party when she was six years old. And all the while, Daniel sighed, waiting for the next obvious question. How many times had he explained himself? And yet, people thought the time-tracking machine worked on its own. It could only show what had happened at the moment the event plaited itself in the memory fabric, but once back to the present day, it was the raw talent in the kitchen that made or broke the day. But to talk about that was to spoil the magic.

"You must have a favorite dish," the reporter insisted with a coy look. "The recipe only your mother could prepare. Would you be able to reproduce it?"

Saved by the bell—or rather by the ringing of his mobile phone—the name on the caller ID made Daniel blanch, and he stood up so fast the chair fell to the carpeted ground with a muted thump. "Please excuse me—that's awkward—an emergency," he said as he walked away, phone to the ear, shoulders down like a rugby fly half about to dash for the opponent's field. "Denise, I'm busy!"

"And top o' the fucking morning to you too, sunshine! I'll be brief. Mum is on the last wish list." Daniel stopped walking. "Dan? You heard me? It's time for the last meal."

"Yeah, what of it? The food reproducers at the hospital are great. I trained the staff myself. Why the fuck are you—"

"I can't explain over the phone, just come up here!" Denise sighed, and he saw her in the back of his mind, Denise with the wiry reddish hair and her freckles, pressing the middle of her forehead with two fingers and counting to ten, grounding herself or else she'd bite his head off over the phone. "Please, just show up. Blame it on me, if you must."

"Oh, you can count on that!" Off went the phone. A deep breath, and then another, and another. He had to come to his senses, hoping the reporter hadn't heard the conversation. It wouldn't look good on the papers if he said he didn't have a childhood favorite recipe, or that he sometimes wished his mother would end her days the way she forced her children to go through their early days: dry toast and water from the tap, greasy food from tins and frozen pots. Why did Denise call him? She knew there was nothing he could do.

The brutality of the memory made him shiver in fear, especially as he saw the reporter at the other end of the restaurant, nibbling on her prawn cocktail, oblivious to the shift going on inside the celebrity time-chef who brought that blissful remembrance to her life once had.

II.

There was the recipe card, yellowed with age, written with the meticulous calligraphy of those who couldn't waste an inch of space on the paper. Manjar dos Deuses, or the Gods' Pudding: a coconut flan served with a dried plum syrup. It was all the rage back in the day, an obvious choice for a supper party at home. Any woman of his mother's generation would have had it at least once, but the cold fact didn't quite match what he remembered of his mother. "Just what memory did they unearth from her hair?"

"The time-cooks said they saw her picking the recipe from a neighbor and then writing it down."

"But they didn't capture her preparing or eating the pudding."

"No, but does it matter? That was the memory in her hair, Manjar dos Deuses with sugar syrup and prunes. This was the recipe I found in her stuff. This is her handwriting. All this work, and she didn't even eat it!"

"Did you eat it?" Daniel couldn't help asking.

"I hate coconut," Denise flinched. "When it's my turn, I'll ask for my mother-in-law's baklava. That's proper food for the gods. Now, then . . . D'you think the cooks could have messed this up?"

Don't tell her what you think, Daniel thought. No use hurting her, it won't fix anything. "Dunno, but it won't hurt me to check, since I'm here . . . " Denise sighed, relieved. *Note to self: make her a tray of baklava when this is over.*

III.

The hospice time-traveling device wasn't new, but it worked well enough. It could produce ten slots per week—a fair number, considering the small clientele. "We don't need the big guns, like those weird museum machineries. We don't go too far in the past. Fifty, sixty years back, tops," said one time-cook. "People like it simple. Mum's special porridge, grandma's pie, nothing fancy."

It made sense: all a matter of perspective. His clients wanted what they had at their honeymoon or on a joyous holiday, stuff dripping with privilege and joy. The last wish brigade merely wanted comfort for the journey ahead.

"I saw her writing the recipe," the time-cook carried on. "A different moment, to be sure, but we have that from time to time: two memories plaited in the same strand, referring to the same dish."

"How old was she, then?"

"Twelve, tops. School uniform, plaited hair . . . "

At the same age Daniel began to cook for himself, because Denise was out working at all hours and mother couldn't be bothered leaving her bed. And even when she did . . . The taste of dry toast still clogged the back of his throat. "Listen, lads, it wasn't your fault," Daniel added, banishing the foul taste away from his mind. "I'm sure you did your best. She's just a tough customer."

"I suppose she is, since she's used to the best in show!"

"Could you show me the rest of the kitchen?" Daniel forced a press-approved smile as the cooks gave him a tour of the facilities. Later, he'd sign toques and books, and pose for pictures with the crew before wasting one of his own time-tracking credits on the hospital's equipment to see his mother writing the recipe for the manjar. His mother—a malnourished, grubby little girl with lice in her reddish-brown hair, holding the black ballpen with the same difficulty she'd have to hold cutlery later in life.

She only had one card—that was why she was writing so slowly. No room for mistakes. When she added the last word, she smiled in bright triumph—and then, little by little, the smile faded into the blue grimace Daniel had been so accustomed to.

When the "beep" signaled the end of the session, he sighed with palpable relief upon seeing the white Formica and gray chrome empty kitchen through the glass door of the time-tracking equipment.

The frown on his mother's childhood face wasn't displeasure. It was a sadness too deep to explore without proper instruments.

IV.

Daniel had expected worse for someone who was on the last wish roll. His mother looked well, given the circumstances—sure, thinner and sallower, but with the usual penciled eyebrows over the same hooded eyes, the same Roman nose both he and Denise had inherited.

"Oh, no, they called the big star!"

The same viper tongue, too. "Top o' the morning to you too," Daniel replied through the press-approved smile, trying to figure out what to say next. "How are you?" was a silly question and "did you miss me" was useless. Denise steered the attention to the plate resting on the plastic tray. "Mama, mama, isn't this nice? Daniel prepared an heirloom recipe especially for you!"

"Fancy that! The celebrity chef made me a dish? Must be my lucky day."

Daniel frowned as he looked at Denise, who had the decency to appear mortified. "Mama, won't you eat it? Daniel prepared it especially for you."

"Where are the cameras? Did you hide the cameras? Am I going to be in one of your silly shows?" When Daniel didn't rise to the bait, the old lady pierced the pudding with a plastic spoon twice and then turned to Denise. "You eat it. I'm too much of a hillbilly to appreciate such finery."

"Remind me again why did I bother?" Daniel turned to his sister. "I wasted my personal credits to see the memory and . . . "

"Blah, blah, blah! Why did you think I'd eat your gourmet crap?" His mother raised her voice. Again, Daniel closed his fists, waiting for the monster behind that sound. "Fancy crap to feed the bling-bling crowd, that's all. I didn't ask for this. I'm not that ill to be given such mercies."

"This crap," he picked up the plate, "is far from refined!" Daniel handed the plate to Denise. "Find someone who likes coconut and give this to them. Don't bloody dare call me again unless it's an actual emergency."

He left without looking back, the memories simmering and floating like fat atop a soup: bread and margarine for lunch if he was lucky; bouillon for dinner if things were well; the laughter of the other children when he ate a tomato the way one eats an apple because he was so hungry, so hungry. His mother refused to cook, refused to even look at the hob, leaving him and Denise to the care of others, leaving them to the care of the wind, forever famished. If someone would ever throw one lock of his hair into the time-traveling device, that's what they would find: a tomato eaten like an apple, and the laughter, the painful laughter that made him a chef: *you'll see, the lot of you, I'll cook my way out of this hellhole, you'll choke on the morsels, just you wait.*

A tomato and the laughter: but they weren't as painful as the memory of his hunger.

V.

"There has to be some secret ingredient. Dunno, something extra or something missing, if you know what I mean. Please, Dan, you can't just give up!"

"I didn't give up. I went there, I saw the memory, and I cooked what I saw. She didn't want to eat it; she never wants to eat anything. Why are you insisting on this? I know all your friends' mothers had extravagant last dishes, but that's not in the cards for us." Denise pressed the center of her forehead. "And stop doing that!" Daniel snapped. "You look just like her when you do that."

"And you think I don't know that? I can't help it. You sound like her, don't you know."

"More's the fucking pity." Daniel looked around his kitchen, all deserted after the night shift ended. The time-tracking device was put away for the night, but it still looked magnificent. It was a state-of-the-art machine that could run twenty slots per day. Not that he needed that much—he didn't have that many clients—but it was good to know he had extra voyages just in case he needed to research a memory further. "Just humor me, did she eat the pudding in the end, or . . . ?"

"All of it," Denise sighed. "She almost licked the plate! But she kept insisting she didn't want it, that it wasn't what she wanted or what she remembered. Perhaps it was all in the way her mother prepared it? Or her grandmother, or some other relative?"

"Denise, stop it. She probably invented a story herself. Think about it. Half a dozen eggs? Whole milk? Shredded coconut flakes? Denise, those things would have been expensive as heck for her family. Remember, rat poor, the lot of them—we heard the stories one time too many. We can't go anywhere nice; we can't have anything nice because they were rat poor and God help you or me if we dared to want more!" Again the laughter ringing in his ears, the tomato pulp running down his chin, and his mother excusing herself, saying her son was soft in the head, *you understand, he got it after his father, bless him* . . . And all the while, she wouldn't listen when he said he was hungry. *Didn't I just feed you? You ask for too much.* "What do you get from this torture?"

"Peace of mind, that's what." She didn't go on, because she didn't need to. Denise was and always would be the bigger person. She was the one that brought home the ingredients he asked for, at whatever cost; she was the first person he fed. For years, she was his only client and only companion, the one reason he kept learning, the one reason to wake up in the morning: *I must make lunch for Denise, I must make dinner for Denise, she can't go to work hungry.*

"I want to make her comfortable. That little girl in the memory . . . There must be something I can do. I know the manjar was special. Trust me, Dan, please. I know it is."

"Fine, fine. But I'd need another sample," he relented. "Cut a strand of her hair and bring it here within an hour, or you best forget it. The machine is excellent, but it has limits."

And so do I, he wanted to add, *and you are pushing them too much.*

VI.

The following morning, moments before the restaurant crew arrived for work, Denise brought a strand of yellowish hair in a paper napkin. It wasn't the ideal way to carry a sample, but Daniel wouldn't say a word about it—or else he'd change his mind once more.

He placed the hair in the acrylic box to the left of the machine, and then locked himself with Denise inside the square-meter-and-a-half green molded plastic traveling cabin. "You will stand as witness," he said when she tried to leave. "It was your idea. You will see how I work now."

Denise tried to leave again, but Daniel pressed a button inside the cabin and everything around them lost color and smell; next thing she knew, she was lurching forward in the small cabin as the surroundings spun, while Daniel remained stable in his corner, a quiet smile on his lips and both feet planted on the chromed ground.

The world outside melted, the modern kitchen became an off-white void that was tinged here and there with spots of verdigris and silver until, drip by drip, a new scenario emerged from the mixing colors.

A concrete tenement hall, dingy gray, and smelling of rancid fat and petrol fumes, stood before the two siblings as Daniel opened the glass door. There: at the staircase, carrying an immense government-issued food parcel, his mother at twenty. No, hold it: that was his grandmother at twenty: his mother was at the door of their apartment, a five-year-old girl jumping up and down with the joy of those blessed with a miracle.

Denise reached out to touch the little girl, but the memory flicked and almost disappeared. Daniel didn't bother telling her the rules of the machinery and didn't bother scolding her. Instead, he ran toward what passed for a kitchen in the bedsit: a camping stove, an ancient icebox, two pans, and two pots. The scene played on: his grandmother putting away the packets of rice, beans, and chickpeas, the sardine tins, and the ground coffee, and then holding a paper packet like a holy relic, a boon from the gods.

Instant pudding.

Daniel would laugh if only he could stop trembling.

Instant pudding reinforced with powdered milk and corn flour to ensure the mixture would be thick enough to be like a true Manjar dos Deuses once unmounded. His grandmother cooked on her knees, while her daughter pestered her with all the great things they would eat now that they received their parcel, and how one day they'd have a nice oven and a sink, just you wait, when Dad came back and the rumble outside was gone.

The paltry war bundle, the soot on the bedsheets that did double duty as curtains, all horrified Denise. But Daniel only had eyes for the little black pot over the camping stove, to the care that his grandmother devoted to the ingredients, the way she quietly stirred everything, oblivious to her daughter and her dreams. The secret ingredient was a small bottle of coconut milk—and after his grandmother emptied the contents of the pot, she filled it with water and shook it to remove even the most recalcitrant dreg.

And his mother ate it all, still chatting about the days to come. Nothing better, nothing nicer in the world: her mother's manjar was the best thing in the world.

He reconstructed the next years in his head. Soon, he figured out, that little girl would find out the Manjar dos Deuses her mother made to please her was a sham. She'd go to school and her classmates would fill in the details and taunt her for her poverty, for the father lost in the rumble, for the lice in her hair. The desire soured, the anger turned into resignation, all inside a recipe card she kept for fifty years, untouched like a museum specimen. Food became fuel so not to be again the knife that her colleagues used to slash her.

The same knife her son branded against her: her brightest enemy, sided with the riches and their glittery banquets that she could only glance at from the window.

Instant pudding? Why would he eat that crap? He'd make the real thing, and eat the real thing, and never be hungry again. He must have told her so, didn't he? Or some words to that effect. They were always shouting at each other, ravenous and angry, one feeling fueling the other.

The scene blurred once more; the colors fading into green, into white, into black, and then reshaping themselves as Daniel's kitchen. Denise opened the door and retched on the floor in a fit of tears while her brother observed the scene with glazed eyes.

There, he thought to himself: underneath the monster that shaped his entire life, a hungry five-year-old girl.

VII.

Daniel and Denise stared at a blue plastic bowl with the white, gelatinous mass faintly smelling of coconut and reconstituted powdered milk, proffered with no introductions or explanations. "You don't expect me to eat this crap, now, do you?" their mother riled them out of habit, but the voice didn't stir up much that time—Daniel kept his hands at his sides; Denise didn't touch her forehead.

"What is it with you two? You poisoned the food? That desperate to get rid of me, are you?" Again, no answer, and she took a spoonful of the pudding. "Jesus, you two, always so bloody stuck-up. Here, I'll eat it, all right, star chef? If that makes your sister happy, I'll eat it."

Something shifted when she ate the spoonful, and it led to another, and then another, and another until she was scraping the bowl, ravenous, desperate for more. And the more she ate, the more she stared at her son and her daughter, and in her eyes their faces were no longer distant and haughty, but human, too human, too close to her heart, too much like what she could have been if only, if only. "How dare you?" turned into "How could you?" and then into "Why didn't you do this sooner?" and "Why didn't I tell you?" until it all dissolved into tears and stomachache. She'd throw the bowl away; she'd howl, she'd try to cuss to make the pain go away—she would if only she could only stop shaking, the longing catching up with her at last.

"It's not like hers," she said at last, attempting to articulate the phrase in the composed, detached manner her children knew her for. "But thanks, I suppose. For the effort."

"Likewise, I suppose," Daniel replied with the same rehearsed tone, knowing only too well that this was the furthest she'd dare to go to acknowledge it all. But when future historians combed through his hair for clues about his story, they'd find that cheap pudding plaited in the strands, and the peace that came with it. It'd have to be enough.

ABOUT THE AUTHOR

Anna Martino is a Brazilian SFF writer and editor, publishing in English and Portuguese since 2013. Her work in English was featured in magazines such as *Strange Horizons, Hexagon, Luna Station Quarterly,* and *Translunar Travellers Lounge,* and was also performed at BBC World Radio. She lives in São Paulo with her husband and son.

The Odyssey Problem
CHRIS WILLRICH

When the sparkling golden glow fades and my skin stops feeling like mites are crawling all over it, the Room is gone, and I am shivering in a vast bright chamber and strange people clad in orange, red, and blue pajamas are asking me how I am. I don't know what to say. I feel lighter, and the air feels cleaner; I am giddy and frightened. The Room is my only home, and now it is gone. Sometimes, in the old times, people would open the door of the Room and someone would stare at me and ask questions. I would never answer. The questions weren't for me but for my jailers. I didn't talk much then. I used to promise to be good, but it didn't seem to matter.

These new people do want me to speak, but I am so bewildered I can't manage to say anything, not even *I am so bewildered I can't manage to say anything*. I am taken through a series of corridors, all blazingly bright and full of calming colors, and finally into a place with many beds beneath machines that make gentle sounds. People in blue wave devices over me and inject me with something. I sleep.

When I wake it still seems too bright, but I feel somewhat better, clearer-headed. I am given food, something like what I am used to in the Room but fresher and tastier. I eat with caution at first, then greed. The water is clean. It is like a dream.

A woman in an orange shirt speaks to me. I look closely. She seems slightly different from the people I've seen before at the door of my Room. It is not just her skin color but the shape of her head. I do not think my language is her first language either. She asks, "How are you feeling?"

"Better," I say.

"That's good. You must have questions."

Do I have questions? I wonder. I have food and drink and space to move. I am clean. People are behaving kindly to me. Questions seem superfluous. But I feel as though the woman in orange has a desire to answer questions. So it is for her sake that I try to form them. "Where I am I? Who are you?"

"This must all seem strange to you. You are aboard the *Odyssey*."

"The-o-di-cy?"

"It doesn't translate well. It literally means the story of a man named Odysseus, a traveler from another world long ago and far away. But the connotation is 'great journey.' My *Odyssey* is a Research-Contact-Diplomacy Scout of the Federated Cultural Republic. I am Captain Temple. Do you have a name?"

"I . . . I don't remember . . . "

"You've been terribly treated; I don't wonder that you've lost that memory. The doctor's begun mental therapies. Perhaps it will come back to you."

"I lived in the Room . . . always."

Captain Temple frowns. "Yes. We've encountered such Rooms several times in this part of the galaxy."

"I don't understand. There is only one Room. The one in . . . " I struggle to recall the name of my home. "Emulvain Town. There can only be one Room. Only one person needs to be in it." I recall hearing this when my jailers answered questions of the people who came to stare at me. "There is only ever need for one Room, one prisoner. I remember that."

Captain Temple's face is strange to me, so I cannot be certain of her expressions. But I think she is angry. It frightens me, but it becomes clear it's not me she is angry at. "Do you understand that there are other worlds? Beyond Emulvain Town and its planet?"

I remember things taught to me before I was chosen for the Room. "Yes."

"There are people on some of those worlds. Some resemble your people as much as I resemble you. Others are very different. They have all sorts of ways of living, and all manner of machines. For example, this vessel is similar in basic concept to the watercraft of your home planet, but larger and much more powerful, and it sails space, not the sea."

"Yes." I remember seeing flags fluttering on the boats in the harbor during Summer Festival, long ago.

"There were once beings as far beyond us as this vessel is beyond your ships. Farther. They were powerful and cruel. They created the Rooms and scattered them on less advanced planets. Each Room has the potential to beam enough energy to power millions upon millions of devices. In time the Room can make a planet a paradise. Abundance for all. No scarcity."

38

"The Room is necessary," I say.

"That's what your people told you, is it? Your world became a utopia because you had a Room. But the beings who made the Rooms gave them special locks of sorts. They can only be activated if an intelligent being is inside, constantly suffering. Like you."

"I was necessary."

"We think the ones who built the Rooms were trying to make a cruel argument about complicity, testing it out on living worlds. The Rooms aren't really for you, they're just talking points in a debate waged by gods." The captain looks away as if sickened. "I can't judge your people, really, but I was able to rescue you. I've rescued and resettled several victims like you. FCR contact protocols allow interference in cases of outside meddling—"

"Captain." A man in blue touches her shoulder. "My patient needs rest."

"I'm sorry," says Captain Temple to both of us. She smiles at me. I think the showing of teeth is meant kindly. "We'll talk later. Get some rest."

"Captain?" I ask, because I know answering questions is something that matters to her, and also because this question matters to me. "What . . . what happens to me?"

"Once we're back from these unknown spaces there are many worlds that would take you in."

"Can I go home?"

The frown returns to her face. "Yes. But it won't be the same. If a living victim is ever removed from a Room—"

"Captain," the man in blue objects again.

"Rest," she says.

My world is on fire. I learn that days later when I am much recovered and free to roam the *Odyssey*. That is why Captain Temple frowned. I see the occasional broadcasts that are still possible with the loss of most of the world's power. When I left the Room my people broke the terms and the Room self-destructed. Civilization toppled like a bunch of toy buildings with the rug tugged out from under them. I am hated by many, celebrated by others. Some even claim me a god who once suffered in flesh, and who has now visited righteous punishment upon the emulvain.

All I am certain of, watching the broadcasts, is that I do not want to go back.

I start learning in earnest as the *Odyssey* leaves orbit to continue exploring the galaxy. (Among the first things I learn is the meaning of the terms orbit and galaxy.) The crew says I can have a place in the Federated Cultural Republic when they eventually return there. At first I'm eager to study to become a ship's crew member. They are very polite about that. I gather that refugees from backward worlds (and I must remember, even if my world wasn't backward before, it is now) often want to become crew. We wish to be treated as special, the only members of our various species who can surpass the dirt and excrement and narrow dimensions of our origins and join the heroes of the stars—as if this salvation was something we had earned. Dazzled, we imagine becoming indispensable to our rescuers.

I still have that feeling when I tour the engine room.

The woman who guides me is wearing red and has devices covering one ear and the opposite eye. Her skin color looks exotic compared to both mine and the captain's. I ask, perhaps rudely, if loss of organs is a hazard of engineering work. She laughs and says the only hazard of engineering work is drinking too much mipsir. "No, I lost an eye and an ear in a battle with demonkeepers," she says as she leads me among angled clear pillars swirling with shades of blue like schools of fish made of moonlight. "There was enough neural damage that prosthetics worked better than regrowing the organs. I'm used to it now."

I choose among my many questions. "You have battles? There were no battles in Emulvain Town. Only in old stories for little children."

"Sadly, kid, we do have battles. Not among ourselves. Arguments, sure. But the planets of the FCR learned long ago that cooperation is better than violence. But it's a big galaxy, and high technology is no guarantee of high morals, as you well know."

"Yes."

She waves a hand. "Out there are cultures that like to impose their will on others. They have no problem wrecking planets in the name of their beliefs."

"Like you did." The words slip out of me as I imagine my planet viewed from space, fires visible on the nightside.

"What?"

"Never mind." I feel I have said something wrong, and for a moment I am afraid they will drag me into a narrow room. *Will I feel that way all my life?* I wonder. But the engineer in red still seems friendly, just confused. I ask, "Can you show me the, the . . . " I am learning many new words, and the ship's Al-Jazari Mechanism whispers new ones in my ear all the time. But I stumble on this one. "Schopenhauer Core? Schoenberg Core?"

The engineer laughs. "Right planet, wrong thinkers! It's called the Schrödinger Core. And sure."

"So the person who invented it was Schrödinger?" I ask as she floats me down a wuxia shaft to the lower levels of Engineering. I am asking as much to keep everyone liking me as to learn new things. And I fear being led to another Room, and the questions distract me from that feeling.

"No, it's named for the Schrödinger Gems that power our Varuwult Drive. But the gems were named for Schrödinger. He was a scientist who helped one of our member worlds first understand many weird phenomena. He's famous for a parable about a cat that's both dead and alive at the same time. The gems are exotic matter with some of that same quality—macroscopic quantum effects—so they got named after the parable."

I focus on the simplest of my questions. "A cat?"

"A small, furred creature. But these aren't cats."

She's brought me to a chamber where we can glimpse, through what seems but surely isn't frosted glass, a set of crystals hovering in a circle of blue lightning. Each crystal seems to shatter and reform so quickly that the fractured and the solid Schrödinger Gems appear superimposed upon each other, broken/whole all at once. I clutch my head and the engineer steers me away from the sight.

"Easy now," she says. "A lot of people get that reaction the first time."

I'm still holding my hands to my head. "Do you—hear screaming?"

"Sometimes people experience that the first few times." She laughs. "The mipsir helps."

"What . . . what was Schrödinger's parable?"

She begins telling me about a cat who is stuffed into a small box, and who may be alive or dead, and is in fact somehow alive and dead at the same time. I lose track of the kindly engineer's explanation and feel tight in my chest. I make polite excuses as soon as I can so I can return to my room. "You're bright, you know," says the engineer as she waves me on my way. "You ask good questions. And you're young yet. If you study hard while you're on *Odyssey*, you might make it into the academy on Haivinth, or enlist." I don't really understand, but I make myself smile at the compliment.

I do study when I get back to my quarters. They've given me what seems to me a grand cathedral, though I'm assured it's just the room of a junior officer who volunteered. Its windows look out on either the star-mottled void or the Varuwult Abyss' seething clouds of color. I shudder for a while, experiencing a strange feeling of solitude and safety. When I do my research I talk to the Mechanism while sitting under a blanket in the corner.

My eyes flutter. Sleep is coming, and I fear my dreams. Abruptly, without knowing where the idea comes from, I ask the Mechanism, "Are the Schrödinger Gems alive?"

"The scientific consensus is no," it replies. It sounds like a soft-spoken teacher from before the Room. "No crystalline life-forms have been discovered. However, certain panpsychist beliefs attach to the crystals. It is known that the Branching Way believes . . . "

It tells me more, but I fall asleep.

When I awaken it is to a blaring alarm, and the light is tinted red. I leave my quarters, and as I've been taught, I ask a panel of glass in the corridor how to get to the captain. Glowing golden arrows in the air lead me through hallways and wuxia shafts to a sort of shadowed steel courtyard with black walls shining with lights and symbols, with a kind of round platform rising at its center like a theater stage. Scores of people mill about on the "street," drawing pictures of light in the air, sparkles around them forming words. I never fully learned to read, but I doubt these words are in my language anyway. Up on the "stage" are more people, also drawing with light. Above it all is what seems a dark dome speckled with lights. I realize they are stars. Covering some of the stars is something that looks like a huge silver moon covered with holes through which green light blazes forth. I soon realize by its motions it is an object outside our ship.

Captain Temple looks down from the stage. "Child! You should go back to your room!"

"I don't want to be alone," I say in a very quiet voice, but somehow the captain understands and beckons me up.

"Definitely a demonkeeper ship, ma'am," says a gold-shirted person in a levitating chair surrounded by glowing displays floating in the air. "Over twenty hooshool from any of their known bases."

"Please use their chosen name for themselves," Captain Temple says. "Even if they're shooting at us. Perhaps especially if they're shooting at us."

"Yes, ma'am. Definitely a Branching Way ship, ma'am."

"We are in a dangerous situation," Captain Temple says as I reach the top. "The Branching Way is maybe a thousand years ahead of us in technology, so every encounter with them must be handled with great care. You need to stay to one side and not get involved."

"What do they want?"

"I don't know yet. They've fired a warning shot but haven't spoken. We've been at odds for centuries. We keep trying to get through to them, but they think we're backward primitives."

A man in red with a surprising number of eyes says, "Captain, they are responding." Looking up, I see the silver surface of the Branching Way vessel covered with strange twisting writing. "The glyphs say, 'We know your mission, *Odyssey*, but you are not welcome here. We will purge the galaxy of the Rooms, and with far less collateral damage. Depart this region.'"

"Reply," says the captain, "'We consider this region free space. And we could help each other. We have destroyed several Rooms already, and we have someone aboard with direct experience of one.'"

I see the writing change upon the Branching Way ship. "They're replying," says the officer in red. "'Send the victim of the Room to us, and we will spare you the indignity of a destroyed ship and a captured crew. You are little better than those who use the Rooms. We will not leave this child in your hands, barbarians.'"

Captain Temple raises her voice. "Send this! 'We are not barbarians. All are cared for in our Republic. There is no starvation, no exploitation, no war. We do not even eat meat.'"

The officer in red's many eyes squint at his display. He says, "They reply, 'You are a hierarchical, humanoid-dominated, tribalistic incoherence. You abandon planets to misery with your contact protocols, when you could do much good. You kill innocent plants with relish when you could easily subsist on artificial food. And you torture the gems in your engines. If you are civilized, you are only barely so.'"

"'Absurd! Just to address one of your claims, even if the gems were living, they, like the plants, would be of such low order their use would be entirely moral. At worst it would be no more immoral than agriculture. Trillions of *intelligent* life-forms depend upon the drive.'"

The officer in red's eyes blink as though catching dust. "They say, 'Enough. Send the child or your ship will be destroyed, and you will all face judgment.'"

Odyssey shakes. Green fires burst from the Branching Way vessel and the space around *Odyssey* is blazing blue.

I can't understand the displays around me, but I can sense that most of the people in this room are terrified. Their hands shake. Sweat is on many a strange brow. Their initially calm voices are becoming a frantic babble.

"I'll go," I tell the captain. "Whatever it is, it can't be worse than the Room."

The captain says, "You would do that for people you've only just met?"

"You hadn't even met me, and you saved me. Of course I will."

"They aren't even humanoid. You may feel very misunderstood and lonely. And despite their claims, I don't know that they'd treat you well."

Alarms are blaring all through this gallery. "Tell them," I say.

Again the glow. Again the feeling that mites are swarming all over me.

I am not alone this time, however. Captain Temple is holding my hand as we appear aboard the other ship.

At first, I think we've accidentally arrived on a planet. We are surrounded by purple trees and an abundance of green flowers. Things like winged jellyfish flit through the air. The blue sky above is filled with holes through which the stars blaze in blackness. I see *Odyssey* through one of them, a tiny white sphere with glowing spindles stretching behind it.

Barely before I can take this in, something gelatinous, many-tentacled, and huge as my quarters on *Odyssey* grabs me and pulls me close, tearing me away from Captain Temple.

"Hug," it says, and one tentacle injects my head in what seems a dozen places. There is no pain, only numbness.

"Let her go!" Captain Temple is demanding.

"Contemplate," it tells her, and she vanishes. Then the thing sets me down gently upon red, straw-like grass.

I take a nap.

I have a dream of being in the Room, shivering in my own filth. A voice comes into my head. It is nothing like the voices of my jailers or their visitors. Nor could it be any of Odyssey's crew, nor the beings of the Branching Way. It is a voice almost not a voice, but more like the afterimage of words written in fire. That is a strange thing because I'd still been learning to read when I was chosen for the Room. It says:

IT IS AS I PREDICTED. EVERY LESSER CULTURE ACCEPTS THE SAME BARGAIN. THERE IS ALWAYS A POINT WHERE THE ILLUSION OF MULTIPLIED JOY BECOMES AN EXCUSE FOR HORROR.

I CONCEDE (comes a response like writing in another hand) THINGS PROGRESSED AS YOU PREDICTED. YET YOUR METHODS PROMOTE THE HORROR YOU DECRY. I WILL STIR MINDS TO OPPOSE YOU IN EVERY SPIRAL ARM AND FIELD OF GRASS. HOLD, ADVERSARY! ONE BECOMES AWARE. LET US WITHDRAW.

Then all is quiet (or equally valid, the thought-image of the words blurs) and in the silence of the dream the door of the Room opens, not upon the dim hallway in Emulvain Town but upon a forest of purple trees. Everything is misty and my heart trembles with a feeling of imminent potential.

I awaken in joy. All seems brighter. It is as if I've arisen, not just from sleep, but from a shadowy distortion of life. Now, my body seems to tell me, the true life can begin.

"How do you feel?" comes the voice of the gelatinous being. It is a fresh and lively sound, like crackling ice. I see it looming over me like a glacier filled with rainbows.

"Better," I say.

"Good. We do not fight except at great need. But our rules allow us to rescue captives. I'm happy to have saved you."

"I wasn't a captive," I object, sitting up. "And you didn't save me. I volunteered to come, to save them. They were kind to me."

"You have a generous spirit. But I'm afraid your understanding is limited. As of yet."

"Captain Temple came with me. She refused to let me come alone."

"That is true and speaks well of her. In her Republic there are beings with promise, portents of better things to come. She is one of them. I assure you we have treated her well."

"You seem to think the people on *Odyssey* are bad."

"Bad? No, child, not 'bad' in their own context. They're a young culture yet. They are still quite singular."

"What?"

"How to say it? Cultures at that stage are focused on numbers as distinct entities, and the metaphor of discrete numbers guides their thinking. They think of sapient beings as purely individual. They also think of sapience as a binary yes-and-no state. You are sapient or you aren't. In fact sapience is a continuum. All matter has a grain of consciousness, and all life has a dollop of it, and the amount of the stuff of intelligence increases as you move along the continuum; plants, to Schrödinger Gems, to complex animals, to one such as you, and on up to the beings in our own Branching Way."

"The gems . . . they really are alive? I wasn't just imagining it?"

"Oh yes. I have given you and the captain a serum that enhances your perception of the mentality of all living things. It will aid you in outside-compassion and inside-compassion. Look without and within."

Each blade of grass has a tiny blossom on it that looks like a white spiral . . . there are clouds beneath the dome of the sky that drift, combine, and tear apart like alien continents . . . fruits hang on purple trees, pale as the moons over Emulvain Town . . . the stalks of red grass are like tall buildings with tiny many-legged black creatures scurrying like strange city dwellers amid the towers . . .

It is like being freed from the Room again. The clouds and trees and grass and creatures have a kind of glow about them that words are unequal to. It is as if natural things had once been all blurred background and now are brightly lit foreground.

Closing my eyes, I try also to "look within." I giggle with delight at what I find. My body is a world full of tectonic inhalation and exhalation, volcanic heartbeats, oceans of blood, electrical storms of nerve endings. And my mind is that world's chief city. There is not a single "me" dwelling there but many. There is a me for every shade of emotion. There is a me who'd belonged to the Room, and who is my will to survive. There is a me who'd known a life before the Room, who is my sense of wonder. There is a me who'd been born aboard *Odyssey*, a me of curiosity. And there is a me here who stands in the midst of all the others. That version of me opens her eyes and says, "I've been trapped. *They* were trapped."

My companion understands. "And now all your selves are free of tyrannies like your planet and like the Republic. And they will multiply and flourish. They are welcome to live in this worldlet, or, if they like, they may leave the rest of you and go where they wish."

"Leave . . . me? Us?"

"You are thinking in terms of an abstraction, child. If a personality wishes to leave its original body we will free it, by giving it a separate body. Many bodies are possible. Even one such as this."

"What does that do to the original?"

"The original mind expands into the void left behind. In time all is well."

I . . . we . . . shiver a little, but the feeling of joy and emancipation is so strong I/we can't be concerned.

"Do you wish to stay?" my companion asks.

"What of Captain Temple and the *Odyssey*?"

"We have ceased our attack. But having stepped freely aboard this worldlet, by our most sacred laws she was entitled to awakening."

"Take me . . . us . . . to her."

"Of course."

I/we ride within the gelatinous being, its translucent organs consenting to shuffle aside for us as I bounce within it. Though it looks like ice, its insides are warm. A natural air tube connects us with the outside. It is snug and pleasant, and my many selves mostly enjoy the ride.

We find the captain leaning beneath another tree, with a being nearby I at first mistake for a thorny bush. Then we see eyes on the thorns and spot rootlike hands and feet, three of each. "She is many!" the thorned being calls out, and my host answers, "This one is many too."

We are bounced out of my host and land on our feet. We go to the captain. Her eyes are closed. "Ma'am?" I say, as we would aboard the *Odyssey*.

She smiles and focuses on us. "It is good to see you again, child. All of us think so. It's hard to believe we feared the demonkeepers. The Branching Way, that is."

"I . . . we . . . know how you feel. Why did you call them that, we wonder? 'Demonkeepers.'"

"We've been afraid of them and 'demonkeepers' sounds sinister. The Branching Way energy source is analogous to a legend from one of our worlds called a Maxwell's Demon. It is a particle of matter they believe to be sapient, and which can manipulate the movements of other particles. In so doing it creates order out of entropy, power out of chaos."

"If it's sapient . . . does it do it willingly?"

"It's *summoned*. How to explain . . . it's summoned out of sapient substrate of the ship itself. It's similar in concept to the process by which a wayward personality is allowed to be taken from a whole person. Have they talked about that? In this case the particle of thought can't be reduced. It is only itself. And as it is born willing to serve, it can't do otherwise."

"Wait!" There is a storm across the world of our body; our skin chills. "So they *create slaves*?"

"You needn't put it so crudely, child. The so-called demons love their work by definition. It cannot be otherwise. And they are happier than we."

Our various selves are arguing, but there is a fragile consensus. "Captain, we have to speak out against this."

"There is nothing to speak out against. Not here. No, it is to our own backward civilization that we must return to, to end the barbaric practice of trapping and torturing the Schrödinger Gems. We cannot look away from that. From there we will fight against hierarchical organizations like the Fleet, and the eating of living things—"

"Plants, you mean?"

"Yes. But first the gems." The captain looks at the members of the Branching Way. "Friends. We ask that you release the part of us that longs to return to *Odyssey*."

"That is its right," says the thorn-being, and it and the captain vanish, leaving us beside the gelatinous being on the hill.

"There is so much wonder to be found," we say, "and so much joy. But we must challenge your use of the Maxwell's Demons."

"That is a naïve way of describing the Bright Joyous Ones."

"Nevertheless."

"You are very young yet. In the Branching Way you will be kept healthy and strong and be freed of diseases and mental turmoil you are not even aware of now. In time you will understand that there is nothing wrong with birthing a being like what you call a 'Maxwell's Demon,' if it is guaranteed joy. It is much better than reproducing in a backward system, where your offspring are bound to know sorrow."

"We can't speak to that."

"You have no grievances toward your parents? They who conceived and birthed you knowing there was a nonzero chance you would be one day fed to the Room?"

We lean back against the purple tree, contemplating its pale fruit. "We don't think they knew any better."

"But you do. Or you will."

"We will stay, friend. But we think we will challenge your perspective. Just a little."

But suddenly something is wrong. There is no red light, no siren, but the wind roars and the flying creatures shriek and scatter and sanguine leaves blow across our view. "We see," says the gelatinous being to the air. "We will take action."

Our icy-looking friend leans toward us, all warmth and rainbows. "There is a crisis."

"Another ship?"

"No, not another ship. A crisis within you."

"What?"

"You are holding a personality against their will. A defiant, contrary one that can never fully accept happiness. By our sacred laws they must be freed from you."

"*What?* You can just *declare* that a part of someone's mind wants to be free?"

"Injustice is injustice, on any scale. The separateness of beings is an abstraction. It cannot be used to justify evil. Once that one is free of you, you can all know joy again."

"We know joy now!"

"You are very young."

Everything goes dark.

There are two of me now, or rather two bodies that look like me. One remains with the Branching Way as they journey through the galaxy on their grand missions. What is beamed back with the captain to the *Odyssey* (that dilapidated scow trapped in this muddy little bay of the cosmic gulf) is, I've come to understand, the part of me that is most contrary. It is simultaneously the part of me that condemns the enslavement of the Bright Joyous Ones and the part of me that forgives my parents for giving me up to the Room. What was left behind knows unambiguous joy.

What do *I* know? (For I am merely an *I* now without my friend's serum.) Perhaps a few things, light and dark.

Captain Temple is not the same. She's been relieved of duty pending a review on her home world. Over mugs of mipsir, we come to understand one another. She once thought herself to stand on an ethical and moral peak, and now she knows it was just a tall hill. She is desperate to claim the giddy heights, and so she will labor to free the gems. It will be a hard road. There will be a resignation, and research, and a movement, and a challenge that may extend past her lifetime. It seems to suit her, this goal.

I, who came from a valley of shadow, find it easier to accept my lowly state. Only once do I suggest to her that the creation of intelligent beings that have no choices may be worse than confining (perhaps) animal intelligences to our engines. And only once do I suggest that the destruction of the Rooms might be more urgent. Her furious gaze is more eloquent than her words. For demons and Rooms do not stand as condemnations of her or her culture. So they do not really matter.

I can't prove my own intuitions, and I am but a sinner from the valley. But I am quite sure that there are, somewhere, mountains of understanding that dwarf those upon which my other self stands. A dream-memory nags at me, a sense that if I could shake off my illusions, I could gaze down upon all those peaks of understanding like a fiery bird on the wing. The memory fades.

Yet a week later I have one more encounter with the heights.

It may be mad coincidence. It may be that I misremember my own thought processes. But it seems to me on the very day I make my choice of future, the beaming room activates of its own accord, and my other self appears on the grid, tunic torn and burned.

On hearing the news, I rush from *Odyssey*'s library to the medical core. I see my mirror self telling the blue-clad doctors, "Our ship ventured into the Gossamer Rift, where none of the Branching Way had gone before. There a Cosmic Child scolded us on our crimes. It told us we erred."

"Was it about the Bright Joyous Ones?" I ask, stepping forward with hands still full of memory crystals from the library.

The other's eyes spear me. "It told us we were criminals because we had the capacity to turn all the matter of our ship into self-willed

Bright Joyous Ones and *did not choose to do so*. So it did it for us." They point a shaking hand toward their body. "Our friends threw us into the long-range beam at the last moment. To find my only home. You."

The other looks this way and that at what I see as a soothing place of healing and knowledge, and what they see as an ancient torture chamber. And neither of us is wrong.

The problem, you see, is ever with us.

I drop memory crystals flickering with labels like signposts to my chosen future: *Emergency Shelters for Planetary-Scale Crises, Principles of Global Power Generation, Basics of Trans-Species Medicine*, and *Low-Technology Agricultural Sufficiency*. I want to envelop my other self with wings.

Like Captain Temple did for me, what seems so long ago, I take their hand. Imperfect flesh to imperfect flesh.

I say, "This is not your only home."

ABOUT THE AUTHOR

Chris Willrich's work has appeared in such venues as *Asimov's, Beneath Ceaseless Skies, Fantasy & Science Fiction, Lightspeed, Strange Horizons,* and *Tales from the Magician's Skull.* His books include *The Scroll of Years* (Pyr, 2013) and its sequels. He lives in Mountain View, California with his family.

Inhuman Lovers

CHEN QIAN, TRANSLATED BY CARMEN YILING YAN

It was never a good sign when Song Mike came looking for me at the end of the workday.

"You, come out here for a sec." He leaned against the doorway, nodding in my direction.

I stuck my head out from behind my computer monitor and looked him up and down. The guy was red around the eyes, his blue-gray chin bristling with stubble. He wore a denim jacket draped over his police uniform shirt with the zipper open; his bulging belly really showed off the food stain stretched over it. Wrinkles covered his trousers. He'd probably spent last night sleeping in the office—no wonder his wife had run off with another man.

I stood up and gestured a hand. "Let's go to the top floor. I need to buy a cup of coffee."

Ten years ago, back when Quanzhou's Citong Port District was still rolling in lucre, the city's budget allowances had seemed inexhaustible. The police chief had bought a pile of recreational equipment and set up a police break area on the top floor. Back then, every afternoon break, everyone would get together and play billiards, fifteen bucks a match. Song Mike would always lose to me. Eventually, he stopped playing. Maybe he decided that losing to the girl rookie was too much of a loss of face.

These days, the game room and gym were a ghost town. Only the coffee vending machine in the corner still saw any use.

I invited him to an espresso and grabbed an Americano for myself. After an entire day of suffering through paperwork, I needed a pick-me-up too.

"I've got a job. Rich lady came calling, saying her android disappeared." Song Mike pried up the pull tab and rubbed at his nose. "Sounds like that kind that's been privately modded."

"That kind?" I raised an eyebrow.

In the Port District, you couldn't own a car on the salary from the police station. Everyone would take up some private detective jobs on their own; the higher-ups turned a blind eye, unless you went too far. Song Mike would sometimes take me on as a partner, especially when he needed to interact with females. He was an old-fashioned man; in some areas, he maintained a rare kind of prudery.

Naturally, I wasn't against the arrangement. Who'd turn down a side gig?

"Looks like that kind of . . . " He fished out his phone, pulled up a photo, and handed it to me.

There were two people in the photo. One was a woman, already crossed into middle age. She was dressed in a camel-colored long coat and pretty expensive-looking shoes. She faced the camera, her smile dispassionate and formal. The missing android stood at her side with a focused expression, staring at its owner's profile. It was extraordinarily handsome, bearing a sense of artistry beyond what could be found in products off the assembly line. This guy couldn't have come cheap.

"Isn't that Liu Yan?" I asked.

The woman in the photograph would have been instantly recognizable to anyone in Quanzhou, with her regular appearances in business news headlines. In recent years, she'd announced her retirement and came to maintain a much lower profile, but she still remained an important figure.

"She says that's her secretary of business affairs. It knows a lot of confidential secrets—that's why she has to have it back." Song Mike gave a dry cough. "I don't think their relationship is as straightforward as she says. She couldn't give me this android secretary's model number. She said it was a private custom model."

"Wow . . . " I was admiring the handsome man in the photo once more, expressing my approval for this lady's taste.

"She arranged to speak in person with me at her home one hour from now," Song Mike said, retrieving his phone. "I think the conversation would go better with you there."

"A rich lonely lady who played with fire and got burned, trying to find her missing android boy toy." I shrugged. "Sounds like good money."

I rose to my tiptoes and chucked my empty coffee can halfway across the room into the trash bin. Perfect shot. I glanced at my watch: "I'll get my things. I'll meet you in ten minutes in the parking lot."

On previous occasions, Song Mike would mutter *if you weren't wearing a dress, who could tell you're a woman.*

But it seemed like he was in a low mood today. He only gave me a glance without saying anything.

01.

Song Mike drove his battered Volkswagen while I sat in the backseat, my laptop bouncing along on my lap. We were crossing the decayed city center of Quanzhou; in the distance, we could see the warm colors of the lanterns of Kaiyuan Temple in the dusk. The Ghost Festival was once more nearly upon us.

Flocks of jobless youths wandered the streets in the fine rain, their fluorescent plastic outfits shimmering. They climbed onto the window ledges of abandoned shopping centers, kicking their long legs and chewing gum. Someone recognized Song Mike's car, raised a middle finger, and spat in our direction.

"Aren't you going to deal with that?" I said, half-teasingly.

"We're not on the clock," Song Mike said, his tone weary. "Besides, what can we do? Beat up this crowd of brats?"

But Bin District on the city outskirts was a completely different world. The sea, surface rippling with the last light of sunset, skimmed past the car window. A line of birds returning to their nests touched down lightly upon the white shore. Here, even the sand had been imported straight from some foreign island. House prices in Bin District had hit six digits all the way back in '72.

And our client lived in one of these villas.

Sadly, we weren't in a mood to appreciate the rare sight of such moneyed scenery. Song Mike had me use the opportunity to look up the client's—Liu Yan's—background.

There was a lot of information on her on the Internet, but most of it came from official business news reports and interviews. There wasn't much we could use. Liu Yan came from humble origins; several rounds of outer space investment in her youth had launched her into wealth. Afterward, she'd left Beijing to quietly live in Quanzhou's Citong Port District, but she still held large numbers of shares in several noteworthy corporations. She'd been married once—her ex-husband Lu Guotao had also been a big name in the business world, only to flee under suspicion of serious business wrongdoing quite a number of years ago. They used to operate as a husband-wife team, yet Liu Yan had miraculously come through the business unscathed, managing to keep her own assets.

I rapidly flipped through the search results, picking out the important bits to read out loud. "I can't find much negative news about her online. Does she naturally keep a low profile or is she just good at PR?"

Song Mike snorted. "How many rich people keep their asses clean?"

After his investigation into that warehouse massacre case several years ago had gotten shut down, he'd been allergic to rich folks.

I ignored him, continuing to look through the sources. "Her ex-husband Lu Guotao has an interesting background. Before he got rich off of asteroid real estate, he earned an MD in neurology, and even held a university teaching position related to AI research. He only went into business in his middle age."

"Mm," answered Song Mike, uninterested.

"They seemed to get along quite well as husband and wife." I looked at the screen; just a bit of searching presented me with photos of Lu Guotao and Liu Yan together in various old news articles. There'd never been rumors of extramarital affairs associated with Lu Guotao. It was rare to see for someone at his tier of wealth.

"Not that it stopped her from getting a robot for her loneliness after her husband ran off." Song Mike sounded awfully bitter.

We'd entered the villa district. Everyone was starting and stopping, presenting invitation codes to the countless security systems.

On either side of the sandstone-paved road were little houses shaded by palm trees. The Chinese redbuds were dropping their flowers, carpeting the ground in decaying red. Liu Yan's house was deep within the lake area, a two-story Western-style house, completely snow-white, with a big terrace to one side extending straight into the bay. Wicker chairs and patio umbrellas were arranged on the terrace, so that you couldn't help but envision those long, idle afternoon hours.

Only the lights in the living room were on.

We sat in the car looking at it for a while, speculating on the overall cost of Chez Liu's security system while we were there. Several stealth surveillance drones patrolled above the roof. Not even the biggest bank in Quanzhou got fancier than that.

"You'd be as safe here as if you lived in a fortress," I sighed. I took out my compact, straightened my hair, and touched up my makeup.

Song Mike had changed into a clean dark blue suit before leaving. I maintained it for him in the changing room at the police station for situations like the one in front of us. After his divorce, I'd taken on the duty of making him occasionally look presentable. Some people in the station gossiped that we'd gotten together, but we understood that nothing like that was going to happen between us. He'd brought me into the profession in the first place; it was natural that we'd take care of each other.

That was all.

Ten or so seconds after we rang the doorbell, the lady of the house opened the door.

Liu Yan looked somewhat younger than she had in the photos. Long, thick raven-black hair fell to her shoulders. Only a few signs of artificial tweaking marked her features, which were worthy of being described as stately and lovely. She'd known that Song Mike would bring a female partner, so she was only dressed in velvet yoga clothes and slippers.

I really hoped that I'd still have a waist as slender as hers when I was in my forties.

"Sergeant Song. Miss Ouyang." She shook hands with us in turn. Her voice was soft and sweet. "I'm very grateful that you'd take the time to help me resolve my little personal problem."

Song Mike nodded.

We walked into the living room and sat on one corner of the sofa. Liu Yan's home didn't give off any of the signs of the nouveau riche. Every article of furniture was expensive in a simple, elegant way. A dry-brush landscape ink painting scroll hung on the wall. Definitely an original, I thought.

Liu Yan personally brought us tea.

I was surprised. A fancy house like this, without a housekeeper.

"Forgive me, normally, these duties would be performed by 3908," she explained apologetically. "After its disappearance—"

"3908?" I raised an eyebrow.

"That's the name of my missing android secretary. It came up with the name itself. I'd wanted to give it a more humanoid name, but it was very stubborn on this point." Liu Yan laughed.

Song Mike and I exchanged a look.

"This is also why I hope to find 3908 as soon as possible. It's—highly intelligent. I'm afraid of it being subjected to suffering and harm." Liu Yan hesitated for a few seconds, her thin hands clasped over her knees. The raised veins on the backs of her hands were the only places where her body revealed its true age.

"Intelligent? You mean, the program in its cybertronic brain isn't the version generally available on the market?" Song Mike asked.

I glanced at him.

He seemed somewhat reckless today, accusing the client of exploiting a legal gray area right off the bat. This wasn't going to help us draw out information. To tamper with an android's cybertronic brain programming was technically a crime but faced with companies' quest for profit and geeks' curiosity, the law was increasingly becoming empty paper.

"That's not important," Liu Yan said, with a faint lift of her head. Her voice rose. "I'm simply saying, you can treat this as a missing person case with a real person. Perhaps it seems absurd to you, but ever since I started living alone, it's been my only companion. I see it as a member of my family."

"We understand how you feel." Smiling at her, I took out a paper notebook and pen—for some reason, the gesture always made clients feel like they were being taken seriously. "And AI inspection is outside of our purview. It's just that we need to understand the logic driving your android secretary's actions to better figure out what happened to it."

Liu Yan's expression eased somewhat.

I stealthily shot Song Mike a look. "Could you describe the exact circumstances of its disappearance?"

"It was yesterday morning," Liu Yan said. She became calm and methodical as she began her recollections. I was reminded that she'd once been a successful businesswoman. "3908 is also my fully authorized business representative. I had it visit the company office to interview a new director of financial affairs. But at the appointed hour, the company called me saying that 3908 hadn't arrived at the meeting room. I was taken aback and concerned. I had my people search the entire route. 3908's car was parked on the frontage road next to the highway near the company. The door was locked. There were no signs of force. It was simply that the android had disappeared."

"Isn't your android equipped with a location tracker?" Song Mike asked.

"Not anymore." Liu Yan shook her head. "It doesn't like having surveillance on its body. I removed the device on its behalf."

I wrinkled my brow.

"Forgive me, ma'am." Song Mike leaned forward. "Just what level of independence and intelligence does your android possess?"

"3908 is the work of an artist friend. I admit, it doesn't run the standard program," Liu Yan said. She didn't seem to mind Song Mike's repeated attempt to intimidate. "3908's intellectual capacity is beyond my ability to quantify in specific terms. After all, I'm not a field expert."

The corner of her lips curved faintly, as if she'd thought of something. "All I can say is that in day-to-day interactions, it's completely identical to a normal human being, simply more innocent. It's a good boy."

"Ma'am, you've really got guts." Song Mike shook his head. "Once the programming goes wrong—"

"To live in this world is to accept risk," said Liu Yan, lifting her gaze. "Next to the impenetrability of the human heart, I'd rather have a robot as a companion."

As police officers who interacted daily with the evils of humanity, we were both wordless for a time.

"Why do you think it disappeared? Who would want it?" I tapped the paper with the point of my pen, breaking the silence.

"I really—don't know." Liu Yan spread her hands a little. "I'm largely retired. I'm only involved with the company in a nominal advisory capacity. My social connections in Quanzhou aren't complicated either. I have no enemies. It's possible that someone kidnapped 3908 under the assumption that it has important corporate secrets in its head."

"It wouldn't have value to someone else on its own?" Song Mike asked again.

"In terms of monetary value, it would be worth a top-tier luxury car, I suppose. My friend's creations have always had very high market value." The corner of Liu Yan's mouth lifted; her smile was a little ironic. "It could be resold after reformatting the brain. It's very beautiful. It could easily find a buyer."

She thought some more, then added, "I've also put out word that I'd be willing to ransom it back for a good price, but as of yet, no one has contacted me."

"Interesting," Song Mike muttered.

After the third round of tea, we said our farewells and left.

Liu Yan escorted us to the gate. A night wind was blowing; her body seemed especially frail under the soft athletic top. I once again noticed how vacant and quiet this whole villa seemed.

"We'll contact you if we find anything," I said, clasping her hand and shaking it gently. Surprisingly, I kind of liked her.

"If it's already too badly destroyed when you find it, don't show me the pictures," she said. She sniffled. Her cool, refined outer shell had abruptly cracked. "Just tell me what happened. Don't let me see the pictures."

02.

"What do you think?" Back in the car, I huddled up to the heater, rubbing my hands together.

That villa was as cold as an icebox. It wasn't even September yet, but I was covered in goose bumps.

Song Mike didn't answer, busy lighting a cigarette.

"Their relationship probably isn't as spicy as we envisioned. She sees that android more like a pet dog," I added.

Or a friend. But instinct told me that Song Mike wouldn't want to hear that word.

Once he'd deep-exhaled two masses of smoke, thoroughly polluting the air inside the car, he gave me a sidelong glance. "Did you really not notice?"

"Ah?" I leaned over, appropriated the lighter and pack of cigarettes, and lit one for myself. "Notice what?"

"That big house didn't have a single living soul inside." He turned the ignition; the old Volkswagen engine coughed to life. "That woman's an android too."

I choked on smoke, nearly hacking out a lung. "No way . . . have androids gotten that realistic already?"

I carefully thought back on how it had felt to shake hands with Liu Yan, the texture of the skin, the warmth, the amount of force exerted. All of it had been indistinguishable from a human.

"Where do you think we live? There are no prohibitions here like there are in the big cities." Song Mike shrugged. "These hyperrealistic products have been out on the market for years."

I shivered a little, not from cold. "Where? Out of the people we see on a day-to-day basis—"

"Where's your mind going?" Song Mike guffawed. "Those replica people look pretty on the outside, but they all act like dopes. It's easy to tell the difference. The one we met today is different—that's a real high-end product. I've never seen this impressive a replica. But there's still some tiny differences if you look—I can't put them into words myself."

"Where did you see the dopey replica people?" I asked, watching him. He averted his gaze.

I thought about it and understood. "You've gone to Shuicai too?"

Shuicai Street boasted the biggest brothel in Citong Port. Every half year, the station sent someone down to inspect the girls' health certificates. I'd gone too, and all I could say was, hell on earth. Row upon row of gene-edited girls, stunningly beautiful and mentally hobbled, sitting lined up behind the glass display window waiting for guests.

Naturally they were healthy, born with a long list of disease immunities. They would live with the ageless faces of young girls until seventy, and only then begin to decline and age.

And they'd be eternally happy, never to ponder the questions that brought pain to humankind.

Compared to me, stressing every day over making rent, I didn't know who ought to pity whom. If they were using robots to replace them—it didn't seem that bad a thing.

Song Mike cranked the car window down a crack, letting out the miasma that the two of us had produced. "Do you have anything else this evening?"

"Hmm?"

"Let's pay a visit to that android maker. He lives in Shijing. No one knows his real name, but they call him the Jiali Craftsman."

Jiali was local dialect for "puppet show." Now that I thought about it, it made a good nickname for a maker of replica androids.

Song Mike knew him.

To tell the truth, I wasn't surprised at all. At Chez Liu, when Song Mike didn't expend energy on interrogating Liu Yan about her "artist friend," I'd known that he had to already know something. Moreover, the nature of this case had turned from "rich lady trying to find her stolen sexbot on the down-low" toward a stranger direction, thoroughly arousing my sense of curiosity.

Aside from that, Song Mike's state of mind didn't seem quite right. I didn't want to leave him to go at this alone.

"Let's go. I don't have work tomorrow," I said.

03.

Shijing after dark was a land of wonders.

More than a decade ago, this had been the busiest place in Citong. Every day, hundreds of mega-scale interstellar cargo ships would set anchor at the port in an unceasing river, bringing with them an infinite flow of cash, new technology, and travelers. Back then, the entire Port District had been as profligate as one of the oil countries from the olden days.

We'd all thought the good times would last forever.

Then came wormhole shipping. Cargo ships no longer needed to dock here. The Port District had deteriorated with shocking speed into an underground market, even becoming a gathering place for outside fugitives and the jobless. I could be wearing a police uniform and armed with a gun, but even during the day, I'd think twice about going here alone.

Coming here with Song Mike, at least, I didn't have to worry for my safety. He parked the battered Volkswagen outside and led me into Shijing on foot. After the rain, puddles had accumulated on the long-neglected surface of the road, reflecting the colorful storefronts on either side of the street. Most were selling bootleg video games and banned substances, with stands hawking vermicelli congee and fried oysters interspersed among them, wafting inviting scents.

As we walked, people kept coming up to him and throwing an arm over his shoulder. Only his strength of will kept him from getting dragged into a bar to "drink a couple." As for me, I tried hard not to stare at the body self-remodeling aficionados. Their electronic organs were exposed outside their bodies, hearts and lungs even painted with fluorescent pigments, brightening and dimming with their breath and heartbeat. Noticing my peeking, they began to whistle. "Hey, these aren't the only parts we've remodeled!"

I turned away my gaze.

"*That* lives here." Hands in pockets, Song Mike gestured with his chin at a large, rundown building.

The windows of the building were pitch-black.

"What grudge do you have against him?" I'd heard the disgust in his voice. I inspected the stun baton hidden up my sleeve; it was black market equipment I'd gotten myself, smaller than a pencil, but capable of zapping a hulking grown man into pissing himself on the ground.

He gave me a sidelong look. "I'll tell you afterward."

We came to the front of the building. The glass door of the foyer had been shattered long ago. A metal grille and an old-fashioned cable lock kept the homeless out.

Song Mike rattled the metal grille. Its creaks were earsplitting in the silence of the night.

"I know you're in there," he bellowed. "If you don't open the door within the next three minutes, I'm coming tomorrow with an arrest warrant."

No sound came from inside the building.

Song Mike and I stood outside the grille. The night wind pierced my outfit.

"He'll come out," he said.

Indeed, a little while later, a flashlight ray brightened the interior of the building. Dragging footsteps approached. I narrowed my eyes; once they'd adjusted to the light, I could see the new arrival. The "Jiali Craftsman" was a small man, hunchbacked and hairless. He wore an old military uniform with no insignia. His face was covered in wrinkles, but his eyes were quick. He could have been anywhere from thirty to seventy.

He opened the cable lock with a jangle of keys, letting us inside. I noticed that his hands were long, white, and slender; the nails were speckled with filth. Up close, he stank of alcohol.

"You promised you wouldn't bother me," he complained in a little voice.

"As long as you behave, I'd naturally have better things to do than deal with you." Song Mike snorted. "Go, let's inspect your workshop."

He hesitated, then took us onto a somehow still-functional elevator to the basement.

The huge space was brightly lit. When I made out the scene in front of me, I had to take a deep exhale to get myself under control, to not scream.

Human body parts lay scattered everywhere. Arms, legs, female chest cavities equipped with variously shaped breasts. Hair of every color lay bundled in the corners like giant stacks of hay. Row after row of faces hung from stands. A little girl was drawing eyebrows on one of them with a pen.

No, that wasn't a real girl either. Upon closer inspection, she was only humanoid from the chest above. Below, her body was a tangled mess of metal supports.

Fuck, it made my hairs stand up on end. I felt cold sweat running over my goose bump-covered back. After nearly a decade as a police officer, I'd seen plenty of murder scenes, but the tableau here was uncanny beyond reason.

This definitely wasn't Song Mike's first time here. He wandered freely between the workbench and the lathe, casually picking up an ear here, a finger there, to inspect.

The Jiali Craftsman stood against the wall, closely watching Song Mike's every move, his hands hidden in his sleeves.

He was afraid of the police.

"I've worked on nothing but fully aboveboard orders of late," he rasped. "A clothing company on Mars requested two hundred stage models. I've been so busy that I haven't left the room."

Song Mike circled back, took out his phone, flicked it on, and held it in front of his eyes. "Did you make this?"

The screen displayed the photo of Liu Yan and the android secretary. The Jiali Craftsman averted his eyes.

Song Mike's knee went right up, landing a heavy blow on his stomach. A series of murky bubbling noises emerged from the small man's throat. He curled up on himself. My brows drew together; I took a few steps back.

"I'll ask you again. Did you make this?" Song Mike yanked his hair.

"They gave me a lot of money. Told me to keep it secret," the Jiali Craftsman wheezed. Reflexive tears had trickled to the tip of his nose, where they dangled, catching the light.

"Stand up and tell me, who ordered it. What did they ask for."

He tilted his head, looking first at Song Mike, then at me. His voice shook: "If I tell, I'm dead for certain. They aren't normal people."

I looked back at him, smiling. Song Mike never beat up innocents. If he thought he could play for my pity, he could think again.

"If you don't tell, you'll be dead with even more certainty." Song Mike smiled, showing teeth. "Don't forget the business at the warehouse. You still owe a debt."

"That woman was the most meticulous work I've ever done." The Jiali Craftsman had gone to wash his face; when he returned, he'd regained his composure. "All they asked for was quality. They didn't rush me, and they gave me plenty of money. They were generous customers."

"When was this?" Song Mike asked.

"Let me think—at least two, no, three years ago. A middle-aged man placed the order. He'd brought a photo with him and asked me to make a completely identical android." The craftsman picked up a segment of metal skeleton from the workbench and rubbed at it, the neurotic gesture reminiscent of an insect quivering its antenna. "I said, if you want it to be completely identical, you'll have to give me more photos. The next day, he sent me thousands of photos in all kinds of situations. Even some very private ones."

I didn't expect that. Song Mike's expression was unreadable.

It wouldn't be easy to get personal photos of Liu Yan. We'd just visited her home. Her security setup was more than enough to keep out any ordinary stalker.

"I quickly put together a first draft prototype for him. After seeing it, he still wasn't satisfied, saying that it wasn't at the level he'd hoped for." The Jiali Craftsman *hmmphed*, tossing the finger segment back into the small bowl on the table. "It's rare that someone expresses dissatisfaction with my work."

"He wanted something that could pass for the real thing?" Song Mike's brow furrowed.

"A few days later, he brought the original woman in," he said. "I was shocked too. I'd assumed that he was some rich pervert trying to make a replacement goldfish for some woman he couldn't have—an ordinary-looking middle-aged woman at that. I didn't expect them to act quite close—like a couple that had been married for a long time."

Song Mike and I exchanged a look.

"The woman looked much older than she did in the photos. She seemed very subdued, as if she were seriously ill. They stayed in my workshop for an entire day. I revised the prototype based on her appearance until both of them were satisfied." The Jiali Craftsman found a grease-stained binder from under the workbench and flipped it open. It was full of photos of stunningly gorgeous young idols. He finally found a particular page within it and handed it to us.

It was Liu Yan, the wealthy matron we'd just seen. In the photo, she was expressionless. Her body below the neck had yet to be covered in skin, so that she resembled a car with the hood up.

"On the day of the order pickup, the two of them came together. The woman was casually flipping through my product photo catalog when she saw a handsome male attendant model. She joked about buying it and giving it to 'the other her' as a birthday present. And the man actually placed the order right then and there." He looked down, picking at the filth under his nails, his voice becoming an indistinct mumble. "They paid in cash."

"And you never wondered why they needed an android to look that close to the real thing?" Song Mike asked. "Seems like you didn't learn your lesson from three years ago."

"I did do a little research into them. They were important people, people I couldn't afford to cross. I took their money and did my work. I didn't want trouble."

"Too late for that," Song Mike said. "That male attendant android ran away. You may have created another murderer."

Another? My breath caught.

"That has nothing to do with me," the Jiali Craftsman was quick to reply. "They only ordered the androids' chassis from me. I gave them two empty shells and nothing more. They said they'd take care of the cybertronic brains themselves."

Song Mike laughed coldly. "You're claiming you had nothing to do with the suppliers of the cybertronic brains? Who did the work at the adjustment stage?"

The Jiali Craftsman put his hands up. "Don't! Don't hurt me. It was all done through email."

We both watched him.

He turned on his computer and logged into his email. I pushed him aside and did the rest myself, making a copy of all the emails between him and the supplier.

"What else do you want? Ask away." He gave a long sigh. "I'm a dead man either way."

Song Mike thought for a moment, then swiped at his phone screen several more times, before showing it to the Jiali Craftsman. "Is this the man who commissioned the android from you?"

The craftsman's brows drew together, his eyes disappearing into their shadow.

"Don't try to claim that you've forgotten. You're an artist specializing in human faces," Song Mike reminded him.

"That ought to be him," he said softly.

04.

"Want to go eat something?" Song Mike asked me, as we exited the building.

I nodded. "You do owe me a proper meal."

In the end, that so-called proper meal amounted to no more than two Cuban sandwiches from the bar. The owner was an old friend and left us a table in the corner.

We didn't talk about the case as we ate.

After the complimentary post-meal sugarcane juice arrived on the table, the first thing Song Mike said was, "Ouyang, this business ends here. I'll split the reward that comes out of tonight with you."

I nearly punched him on the spot—in terms of physical combat, the bastard really might not be able to best me. Maybe my expression was overly savage, because Song Mike sighed. "It's too late, isn't it."

I crossed my arms, glaring at him. "This has something to do with that warehouse case, doesn't it."

Song Mike was taken aback.

We fell back into silence. He waved his hand and ordered a shot of Jack Daniel's. Few people knew that Song Mike had a pitifully low alcohol tolerance. After this shot, I might have to find someone to carry him back.

"It's Lu Guotao again. Of course it's him." He grinned, gaze fixed on the bubbles slowly rising through the murky alcohol. "Ouyang, how much do you know about the warehouse case of '78?"

"A bunch of hooligans were brawling in a warehouse in the Port District when someone opened fire, resulting in thirteen deaths." I paused, then added, "After you investigated the case, you went from the rising star head of the investigation squad to a neighborhood bobby. I won't relay all the rumors that flew around the station."

At the time, I'd gone back to police school for advanced studies. When I returned to the station, I'd found my partner demoted, and I myself transferred to desk work for no apparent reason. Everyone else said that Song Mike had dragged me down by association. He and I had never openly discussed the business. If he wasn't going to volunteer, I wasn't going to ask.

The warehouse case was like a knot of silence between us.

Song Mike continued to stare at his drink. I didn't rush him. I'd waited this many years already; what was a few extra minutes? Under the dim lighting of the bar, I suddenly realized how much he'd aged.

"In August of '78, I was still in the investigation squad. Someone called the police saying a bad smell was coming from a warehouse in the Port District. I took the team down. You weren't in Quanzhou at the time... good thing you weren't." Song Mike laughed humorlessly. "The scene looked like what you just saw in the Jiali Craftsman's workshop. Only, all the bodies were real. All the pieces of bodies, more accurately. They were already rotting. We called in the coroner and cleaned up for a week. We confirmed there were thirteen dead, all of them unimportant hoodlums from Shijing District."

"Firearms couldn't have caused that level of carnage. How did they really die?" I asked softly.

"That's the strangest part. Aside from the DNA of the deceased, there were biological traces from only one other person at the scene, and they weren't even from blood. Eventually, we found that the fourteenth person on the scene was the Jiali Craftsman. Does that chickenhearted bastard pissing himself on the spot look like he could kill thirteen young men?" Song Mike said, "The deceased looked as if something had straight-up torn them apart. It took Old Li the coroner a lot of work to piece them back together for burial."

"With a case this big, how come I never heard of the Central Office getting involved? Even most of us in the station haven't heard about the investigation," I said.

"It's the Central Office that buried it." He shrugged. "It's not like those Shijing poors had friends in high enough places to stick up for them. They died. So what."

"Do you suspect that someone was debugging illegal androids in that warehouse, and there was some kind of accident?" I recalled his words to the Jiali Craftsman, *you still owe a debt*, and his jab at Liu Yan earlier: *you've really got guts.*

And, Lu Guotao had once been an expert in artificial intelligence. The pieces of the puzzle were coming together.

"That piece of crap was already pants-pissing terrified, after personally watching those androids go berserk." He turned the glass, wiping a sweaty hand on his clothes. "No point in arresting him. In the end, the Jiali Craftsman is only a craftsman—all he knows how to do is make the outer shell. The cybertronic brains came from someone else. His only contacts would've been low-level intermediaries in the organization—it would've been those same people taking away the out-of-control androids and leaving us only the floor covered in corpses. Poor young'uns. They'd probably only come there that day to shift cargo for a bit of spare change."

I stared at the yellow dregs in the glass, a bitter taste rising in my throat. When I compared the timing of several matters, I suddenly understood a whole lot of things. "And Lu Guotao had something to do with this? He kicked this hornet's nest and had to flee?"

"Of course not." Song Mike laughed aloud. "The upper-level officials of Quanzhou wouldn't cross this pack of rich elites for just thirteen poor people. Lu Guotao was forced to flee because of something else, something a lot bigger."

I fell silent. Ever since the decline of Quanzhou, the local government had waited hand and foot on the wealthy who'd come here with their massive fortunes. The local transportation industry had long since gone kaput; the entire city subsisted on the cake crumbs they showered down.

Song Mike had plenty of flaws, but he was a good cop. I could imagine him latching his teeth into his opponent and refusing to let go. I was forced to laugh painedly. That demotion all those years ago now had a logical explanation. And his reason for telling me to extricate myself from the business had also become apparent.

"After Lu Guotao fled, I thought the business was finished. I couldn't do anything even if I wanted to," Song Mike said. "But now it looks like he and his wife Liu Yan remained in close contact. It's very likely that he continued to control business affairs in Quanzhou through her."

"Through Liu Yan's android," I corrected him. "According to the Jiali Craftsman, Liu Yan was involved in the creation of her android replica from start to finish, and she seemed seriously ill already. Do you think—the real Liu Yan's still alive?"

"I'll bet five bucks she's already dead." Song Mike said, "Any sickness they can't cure with all that money has to be something really hopeless."

"Agreed. I think she's dead too." I slowly organized my thoughts as I spoke. "Lu Guotao was secretly researching cybertronic brains this whole time. After he fell afoul of the law and fled the country, he continued to run his business through Liu Yan. Several years later, Liu Yan developed a terminal illness. As her death approached, they decided to make a Liu Yan android who could pass for the original in order to maintain their operations."

After more consideration, I added, "They gave the android an android pet of its own. It's a heck of an arrangement."

Song Mike eyed me. "Maybe they didn't want the fake Liu Yan to come into contact with too many outsiders. The risk of discovery adds up over a long period of time. To have a lonely rich lady's android boy toy show his face as her representative is much more reasonable. A safe chain of puppets."

I looked down, picking at the scraps of lettuce on the plate. "So, you knew from the start that Liu Yan is Lu Guotao's ex-wife, and that Lu Guotao has dirt up his ass crack. Then why did you accept this side gig—unless you were hoping to follow the lead all the way up to Lu Guotao, arrest him, and conclude the case."

He didn't say anything.

I continued, "I have an even bigger question. Why would Liu Yan's android—in other words, Lu Guotao, who's behind everything—ask you to find the missing 3908? He has the money to just commission a new android from the Jiali Craftsman. We can forget that sentimental bullshit about the android being a companion and family member. Lu Guotao is a cold-blooded businessman; he'd equip 3908's brain with some mechanism that would let him remotely wipe its data in case of emergency. And he definitely knows that you're the cop who insisted on pursuing that case all those years ago. He should be avoiding you like the plague."

Song Mike continued to refuse to meet my gaze.

I could hear my voice rising the whole time, unable to control my anger. "Buddy, this is a fucking trap. Don't tell me you can't tell."

"I'm not trying to be some kind of goddamn hero," he said at last. His voice was raspy. His stubby fingers gathered the short greasy hair from his forehead and pushed it back.

I raised a brow.

He lifted his gaze, which crossed my shoulder and fell on empty distance. "Lu Guotao knows that 3908 may have gone rogue. It's more than he can handle himself. He's afraid of a repeat of the incident at the warehouse, with more than hoodlums for victims. I'm one of the few people who know just how bad things can get."

He used the last of his drink to water the decorative plant by the table. Song Mike said, "He doesn't want to retrieve that boy toy android. He's just letting me know, it would be great if I could help clean up a big-ass mess."

05.

Leaving the bar that early morning, before parting ways with Song Mike, I half-bullied him into an agreement: he wasn't going to chase after that potentially already berserk human-passing android on his own.

He agreed with a laugh, suspiciously quickly.

But as I watched that battered Volkswagen drive away in fitful zigzags, I understood there was nothing I could do. I knew almost nothing of the details of the warehouse case he'd investigated. What he'd described tonight was only the tip of the iceberg for sure. In Song Mike's eyes, I would always be that little intern girl. He wanted to keep me out of this dangerous business out of some stupid straight man sense of pride.

Lu Guotao.

I said the name to myself silently as I returned to my cramped apartment. It was already two in the morning. I lay on the bed for half an hour, my eyes closed in vain. All I could think about was the scattered body parts in the workshop.

Irritably, I rose, grabbed my laptop, and sat with crossed legs. Song Mike had told me that Lu Guotao had been forced to depart for other lands for some other business that he couldn't cover up. His wording had been suspiciously vague. Since I already knew Lu Guotao's name and the timing of the case, it might not be too hard to find some leads.

I brought up my phone log and found the numbers of several Central Office high-tech crime investigators I'd met in police school. While I waited for someone to pick up, I logged into the department's internal news network and began to slowly sift through the information.

06.

"Old Song?" I banged hard on the door.

I waited for half a minute, but there was no response.

I went straight to verifying my identity on the retina scanner and entered Song Mike's office. A long time ago, I'd been his assistant; he never removed my access permissions after my transfer.

The interior smelled of cigarettes. I turned on the ventilation fan and went around the room, making an inspection. The old dossier on the warehouse case lay on the table, flipped through so many times that the edges were curling up. The desktop computer was still powered on. I gave the mouse a shake. A password pop-up appeared on the screen.

Never mind.

His jacket and car keys were missing.

I swore. The bastard had purposefully ditched me. This morning, I'd sent him the information I'd put together and left him a voicemail, telling him to wait for me to arrive at the office. Lu Guotao wasn't just some mad scientist who'd played with fire and caused the one-off tragedy. If he'd lived last century, before the death penalty was abolished, the crimes he'd committed in the course of his private research into human-passing cybertronic brains would have earned him a hanging.

Even though Song Mike had been tracing Lu Guotao's tracks for years, I still wasn't sure if he knew just how terrifying his opponent was. Song Mike was an old-school cop. He wasn't much good at digging up and collating online resources. And after the higher-ups shut down the warehouse case, he couldn't have gotten the help of the station's technicians.

I'd rushed into the station and still been too late.

I could picture how he'd look explaining, *I can't take a woman to capture a berserk killer robot*. Heavens, it had been years since he left the front line, and I hadn't seen him partake in any physical training. Chances were he couldn't even outfight a street hoodlum anymore.

I pulled out my phone and called the station's car modification aficionado. "Section Chief Zhang, let me borrow your car."

The other party agreed readily.

As I drove into the hills, I rejoiced in my decision to borrow a car. The smooth highway had quickly become pitted cobblestone. The city no longer had the money to maintain these distant stretches of the public road network.

Song Mike didn't pick up any of the calls I made en route. For my part, I tried diligently not to think about the crime scene photos in the dossier for the warehouse case.

Fortunately, I soon spotted his battered Volkswagen parked crookedly on the frontage road.

I stopped the car and felt for my gun. *When shooting an android, aim for the stomach, that's where the power source is*—silently repeating my freshly gained knowledge once more, I kicked open the car door.

"Old Song!" I yelled.

My surroundings were dead quiet. Pebbly beach stretched from either side of the highway, from which rose massive boulders. Some kind of invasive species with yellow flowers grew everywhere amid the cracks in the stone.

"I'm here," he answered, a hint of resignation showing in his voice. "Didn't I tell you not to come?"

Exhaling in relief, I followed the voice past several boulders and saw Song Mike.

He was crouched beside a man's corpse. No, it was a destroyed android.

3908 was still dressed in the expensive tailored suit he'd worn the day he disappeared. The shirt was pulled open; the power module in the abdomen was gone. The once-exquisite face was in ruins, as if someone had wildly hacked at it with a knife. The Jiali Craftsman's heart would ache at the sight, I thought.

"Is the damage to the face to prevent somebody from recognizing it?" I crouched down next to him. "There isn't much point to that, is there? He's probably the only high-end hyperrealistic male android in the entire Port District."

"It wasn't me," said Song Mike. "It was already like that when I found it. I feel like the vandal desecrated his face more out of jealousy."

"Who would be jealous of—" I fell silent, then shook my head. "My god."

Song Mike stood. "I suppose you came at just the right time. Help me dig a pit and bury it. If someone sees it, takes it for a human corpse, and reports it to the police, it'll be more trouble."

"So you forget that I'm a woman when you need physical work done?"

Together, we cleared out a shallow pit in the pebbles and shifted 3908's corpse into it. The android's cybertronic brain had been removed too, leaving only an empty skull cavity. As I picked up rocks and set them over it, I heard the faint squeaks of metal rubbing against plastic.

Finally, I found a distinctively patterned squarish rock and set it at the head of the grave. Then I took a few steps back and took a picture with my phone.

Song Mike eyed me. "Wanting to give Liu Yan closure? You know we can't—"

"Don't be such a bastard." I sighed, "I know."

07.

We were silent the entire drive back.

Song Mike came with me to return the car key. He made a circuit of the station; maybe he saw that my expression had relented, because he finally dared to say, "Let's talk on the rooftop?"

The rooftop deck was deserted. An autumn rain was falling, drumming against the awning. Water drew trails down the walls.

"How did you find 3908?" I cradled a cup of hot chocolate, letting the steam warm my stiff face.

"Lu Guotao wanted us to find the body. He put the location tracker back in." Song Mike's voice was raspy. He didn't buy a drink; he went straight to lighting up a cigarette. "Yesterday, I got the signal frequency from the Jiali Craftsman. Lu Guotao basically handed me 3908's location on a platter."

He paused. "And how did you follow me?"

I hesitated but told him the truth. "I tracked your phone."

"Motherfucker," he laughed. He didn't sound like he minded.

"I'm really worried about you."

He awkwardly scratched his head. After a long silence, he forced out a mutter of apology.

I shook my head. "Last night, I got into the traffic monitoring database and found the footage of 3908's disappearance. Lu Guotao took 3908 himself. I was terrified, convinced that Lu Guotao was setting a trap to silence you. He'd do it. He's that kind of person."

"I know." Song Mike ground out his cigarette stub under his foot. "I made a faulty assumption too. I only realized when I saw 3908's corpse. Lu Guotao's using me not to clean up that robot boy toy, but his robot wife."

"Why can't he do it himself?" I raised an eyebrow.

"Heaven knows. Maybe he can't bear to. After all, the damned things look too much like real people." Song Mike shrugged. "Tonight, I've arranged to see Lu Guotao in person, right at Chez Liu. We'll see this business to the end. You bring your gun too."

"And he has the guts to come?"

"I told him, if he can't bend his dignity enough to talk things out in the open, I'm not going to take on this business." Song Mike shook his empty pack of cigarettes as he spoke, then tossed it irritably into the rain. "When his fake wife goes insane in the middle of all those villas and mauls one of those leading citizens, he can try cleaning up the mess himself."

I took a sip of hot beverage and closed my eyes. The comfort brought by sugar content was better than nothing.

"Say, do 3908 and Liu Yan realize they're androids?"

"Does it make a difference?"

"I don't know."

"You can't hesitate." Song Mike turned to me, his voice hard. "There's no room for discussion in this business."

I sighed and promised him, "Of course, tonight we'll take care of all the dangerous androids. They're all massive threats to public safety. I've seen the dossier on the warehouse case. I know."

He watched me. "They only look like humans. Don't you get sentimental."

I sighed.

08.

Song Mike remained the driver for our second time going to Chez Liu. I leaned back in the backseat, caressing the handgun in the inner pocket of my jacket. I felt that cold metallic weight right in the pit of my stomach.

I'd brought bad news to plenty of people before. The unspoken rule of the police station: maybe sending a kindly looking woman to bring ill tidings would ease the blow. So I've knocked open door after door, telling mothers their children have died in car crashes, telling wives their husbands have gone to prison.

In the present situation, I only needed to tell one robot that its robot buddy wasn't coming back. I didn't know why I felt so sad.

Their emotions were nothing more than a chunk of computer program. And any grief wouldn't get to last very long.

I closed my eyes, thinking of Liu Yan again, that elegant, fragile middle-aged woman, that moment of loneliness and self-mockery in her expression. It was all fake, all programming. Sooner or later she'd devolve into a killer machine. She had to be eliminated. Privately, I hoped that Song Mike could do the dirty work, leaving me only the duty of helping him take care of the "fake Liu Yan"'s remains, the way we'd buried 3908.

But instinct told me that Song Mike might not be able to do it. He was an old-fashioned man. To have him shoot an innocent woman in cold blood might be asking too much of him. But someone had to do it.

Once again, I checked the number of bullets in my gun.

In the rainy night, Liu Yan's villa looked like a glistening, exquisite toy model, luminously white.

We parked on the little slope behind the house. Song Mike looked several times at his watch. Finally, there came the quiet rumble of an engine in the distance. It was a familiar black Audi. We'd both seen it in the surveillance footage.

"You stay in the car," Song Mike said.

That was what we'd planned previously. I nodded.

He got out of the car. Lu Guotao climbed out of the Audi too. Compared to the photos of him from before his disappearance, he'd gained weight. His long, angular face had become round and kindly. The hair at his temples had become completely white.

"Sergeant Song," Lu Guotao said.

"I don't want to shake hands with you," Song Mike said, coming to a stop several paces away from him.

Their voices came through from the miniature microphone on Song Mike with a rustle of static.

"I understand. I've created many difficulties for you." Lu Guotao let his hand fall, nodding. "Today, I have to ask something of you yet again."

"How do I know that after I wipe your ass this time, there won't be another time? There might be no end." Song Mike said, "Are the police for you to play games with?"

"There won't be another time," Lu Guotao said, sliding his hand into his pocket.

My breath hitched, but the businessman only took out a pack of cigarettes. "Liu Yan and 3908 are special. I have no plans of continuing research on cybertronic brains on your turf. That business at the warehouse proved—sufficiently instructive."

"Explain," said Song Mike.

"The problem of high-complexity cybertronic brain and chassis coordination has never been solved. They lose control. My team and I have tried many ways to stabilize the psyche, with only short-term effectiveness." On this subject, Lu Guotao spoke with a new liveliness, like all people talking about their beloved calling. "If the cybertronic brain is supplied with large quantities of a living person's memories as a basis to operate upon, it's capable of functioning normally for between three and five years, at least in the simulations. It's a pity that there's no way of extracting a living person's memories nondestructively with current technology. We spent money to find a considerable number of terminally ill patients to serve as volunteers. They were happy to leave their families a bountiful inheritance."

I felt disgusted.

Lu Guotao made it sound so nice, but in truth, his test subjects went far beyond "volunteer" terminally ill patients. The scandals that had erupted from several extraterrestrial orphanages were the real reason he fled as a fugitive years ago. Seeing the postmortem photos of those children in the dossier, I'd understood that there was no humanity in him.

"What a philanthropist. I'll say thanks on behalf of those patients. And then you discovered that your own wife didn't have long to live?" Song Mike interrupted.

"Yes." Lu Guotao admitted, unperturbed.

"What did she catch?"

"A type of sequelae from space radiation. In the early years, while we were speculating on asteroid plots, she was the one who'd go out and inspect the land in person." Lu Guotao laughed painedly. "Who knew that karma would be waiting for us twenty years later. She knew that she didn't have much time left, so she brought up using her memories to make an android replica who could appear in person to continue running our business. Initially, I didn't agree. It was like—"

His expression twisted. He made a gesture. "Facing my wife's resurrected corpse."

"I'm sorry for your pain." Song Mike's tone was flat. Even a wall could hear the sarcasm in his voice.

Lu Guotao, too, may have realized that the one standing across from him was not a suitable audience for his angst. He gave a cough. "But we had no other choice. I was on the lists as a wanted criminal. The risk of hiring someone else as a proxy was too great. We found the Jiali Craftsman together and commissioned her body double and a male assistant."

"The assistant was made using a live person's memories? Where did they come from?" Song Mike asked.

Lu Guotao lowered his head. The faint light from his cigarette illuminated his face. He looked much older than his true age.

"3908 is my replica."

"You just said, there's no way of—" Song Mike's brow furrowed.

"I accepted the risk of brain damage. After the surgery, I experienced frequent episodes of epilepsy, short-term memory loss, and difficulties with emotional regulation." Lu Guotao laughed. "But I had no other choice. If I used anyone else's memories, the replica wouldn't dedicate himself wholeheartedly to my interests."

Song Mike was for a moment struck silent. I, too, was stunned in the car. 3908's corpse lying on the rocky beach. And that ruined face. Song Mike had said that kind of malevolence came from jealousy.

Lu Guotao had killed another version of himself?

"When the android version of Liu Yan first powered on, the relationship between us was very awkward. She didn't in fact know she was an android. We periodically revised her memories, wiping out all the continuity errors, helping her maintain a stable worldview." Lu Guotao leaned against the car door, his words light yet urgent. "Intellectually, she knew she was my wife, but it was clear she no longer loved me. I could see it in her eyes. In the process of converting a living person to a machine, something had been lost. At first I thought that a cybertronic brain was simply incapable of emotion. Our goal was nothing more than to keep our business running. The woman who'd lived a lifetime with me was already dead."

He laughed shrilly. The sound covered me in chills. "But she was too fucking similar to Ah-Yan. Every time I saw her, it felt like she'd never died. I wasn't *so* insane that I wanted to sleep with a pile of metal and plastic—we maintained a business relationship. All the way until about a year ago, when my team and I inspected Liu Yan and 3908's memories and discovered they'd fucking fallen in love."

"Oh," said Song Mike.

"I'm not so far gone that I'd be jealous of the robot version of me. Don't look at me like that, I'm no cuckold. My wife's been dead for years. Besides, it's only natural that a robot version of me and a robot version of Liu Yan would fall for each other a second time."

Lu Guotao shrugged and pinched out his cigarette. "But this introduced difficulties to our work. They couldn't have a romantic relationship. The Jiali Craftsman didn't include the capacity for lovemaking on

75

the chassis he made. Who could have thought of a situation this crazy? Every time they tried to sleep together, they'd discover that their bodies didn't match up with normal people's. We were forced to regularly clear out entire chunks of their memories, to keep up their illusions of being real people."

"It was too inconvenient, so you decided to get rid of 3908."

"Inconvenient? I wrecked myself to create him." Lu Guotao's voice rose. "Cybertronic brains can't take this kind of repeated manipulation. Their systems were only meant to remain stable for three to five years originally; with this whole business added in the mix, they've both reached the brink of obsolescence. It's time for those two to retire. I got rid of 3908 myself."

His voice shook. He couldn't continue.

"But you couldn't bear to kill Liu Yan," Song Mike continued for him. "So you thought of me."

"One last time. Whatever you want, I can give you. Money. A promotion. My connections in the Port District can still accomplish a thing or two." Lu Guotao said softly, "I won't make a new Liu Yan. She ought to rest in peace. After resolving this business, I'll leave Earth. You'll never see me again."

Song Mike *hmphed* softly.

Their silhouettes were like two barren tree trunks in the night rain.

"You go to the villa to take care of Liu Yan. Leave things here to me," Song Mike said to me through the communicator.

I assented, hopped out of the car, and went walking toward Chez Liu beneath the hill.

When I'd walked about a hundred meters, I heard the sound of a gunshot from behind me.

09.

Seeing her for the second time, I couldn't help myself—I closely observed her eyes, her hair, and her chest, which faintly rose and fell as she breathed.

The Jiali Craftsman was truly preternaturally skilled.

Liu Yan noticed my gaze. She laughed and shifted aside to let me in. "You know now."

She knew that she was an android.

• • •

"Our conversation likely won't take long, so I won't invite you to sit," she said. Today she wore a light beige hemp shirt and leisure pants. Her hair was plaited behind her head in a Greek-style updo. She'd put on light makeup.

We stood on the carpet of the living room, looking at each other wordlessly.

"Old Lu took care of 3908?" Liu Yan asked, looking down.

"Yes," I admitted.

How much did she know? Would she resist at the brink? I remembered the crime scene photos from the warehouse incident. Cold sweat trickled down my back.

"He didn't suffer, did he?" Liu Yan said in a small voice.

Your husband gouged his face off, I thought. I dug out my phone and brought up the picture of 3908's resting place. "No, he only removed the battery. We gave him a burial. No one will disturb him."

"Old Lu would have also destroyed his cybertronic brain. It's the only way to be safe." She fixed her gaze on that deserted rocky beach for a long time. Then she hesitated, before saying, "In a moment, I hope you'll take care of me in the same way."

For a moment, I didn't know what to say.

"I have many of Liu Yan's memories. I know that androids like us must be eliminated at a certain date, or we go mad." As she spoke, the faint lines around her eyes drew together from her smile. "Finding you two was a plan Old Lu and I came up with together. Old Lu couldn't bear to kill me. He would put it off, day after day, until the point of no return."

So she'd taken care to pretty herself up today. She'd known that her death was approaching and wanted to end things looking presentable.

"Where do you want to . . . " I said.

"How about the garden? Liu Yan loved taking care of the garden best when she was alive. It makes things easier for you, too. I've already had someone dig the pit." Her lashes fluttered. "I weigh one hundred thirty kilos now, as a woman of steel."

10.

"You're done?" Song Mike asked.

"You dumbass." I shook my head.

Lu Guotao's corpse lay on the hill. Half his head had been blown off. Song Mike hadn't used a gun from the station. Thank heaven and earth, he could still keep the finer points in mind.

"If you want to turn me in when we get back to the station, I won't blame you," he said. He tried to light a smoke in the rain, probably thinking he looked like some kind of cool loner hero.

Sadly his lighter wasn't the quality of Lu Guotao's. He tried several times without success.

"Shut up." I grabbed the legs of the deceased. "Come over and help me carry him."

Song Mike was taken aback for a moment, then hurried over. Together, we packed Lu Guotao's corpse into the back trunk of the Audi and drove it to Chez Liu. Earlier, I'd already found the controls for the security system inside the villa and turned off the alarms.

When it came to arranging the scene of an accident, no one was more professional than the police.

Lu Guotao had sought to destroy the robot wife he'd created, only to be killed by the rampaging android. A perfect story. To create a suitable effect, we shot a few more times at Lu Guotao and Liu Yan's corpses. I felt sorry for Liu Yan, that she wouldn't be able to rest in peace under the swaying roses in the garden sepulcher she'd arranged for herself.

But it was the best we could do.

We spent the return trip covered in blood and too exhausted to move a finger. Fortunately Song Mike's battered Audi had an autopilot system; otherwise, with our shaking hands, we probably would've crashed to our deaths against the highway railing.

Several times, Song Mike tilted his head to look at me, wanting to say something but stopping himself.

Tonight, I didn't have the energy for more guessing games. Song Mike's fixation on the warehouse case over so many years had stemmed from more than a sense of justice; he had to have personal reasons. It didn't take a genius cop to guess that.

"The thirteen people who died in that warehouse. They included your friends," I said.

"My brothers," he admitted, "And three boys I knew as a kid. I grew up in Shijing. I changed my identity so I could pass the civil exams and become a police officer. No one else knows."

I nodded. I'd guessed all of it. "That Lu guy got what he deserved. His body count has hit three digits in the course of his fucked-up research. If we didn't stop him, he'd just keep going. We were right to off him."

Song Mike said nothing.

Whether he'd decided to shoot Lu Guotao after seeing the dossier on the orphanage disappearances, or planned it from the start, I didn't want to ponder further. I was certain of only one thing: the world was safer with Lu Guotao six feet under. We were the police. It was our duty.

"You're right. He deserved to eat a bullet." At last, Song Mike covered his face and chuckled roughly. "I owe you big time."

Epilogue.

Outside the car window, the rain continued to fall, raindrops tracing twisted tear tracks on the glass.

I supposed that was another extraordinary thing. In life, Liu Yan and Lu Guotao were a pair of selfish bastards who'd endangered other people's lives without a care. But reincarnated into machines, they'd become a pair of endearing lovers who'd tried to prevent harm to innocents and went willingly toward their deaths.

I touched the contents of my pocket: a little strand of black artificial hair and a ring.

Once things settled, I was going to visit that rocky shore one last time. The robot version of Liu Yan had hoped that a part of her could be buried with 3908.

Once I completed this task, I should finally be able to forget her eyes.

Originally published in Chinese in *Galaxy's Edge* #007, November 2020.

Translated and published in partnership with Storycom.

ABOUT THE AUTHOR

Chen Qian was born in Shanghai and works as a restorer of historical relics. Her books include a short story collection, *The Prisoner of Memory,* a YA novel, *Deep Sea Bus,* and a YA short story collection, *Sea Sausage Bus.*

We Built This City

MARIE VIBBERT

Every sunset, Julia climbs the city her mother built. It feels enormous, on the outside. Inside, it's cramped, a human anthill. It didn't used to be, but Julia doesn't remember what it felt like when there was room enough for everyone.

In the locker room, Rafael's elbow scissors into her personal space as Julia zips her coveralls. Her helmet and face shield are grimy, the padding smells of a mixture of her sweat and the false sweetness of institutional cleaner. The breather elastic is way too loose. She's already tied knots on each side.

Rafael stays too close, his chin tucked down. "They're talking about cuts. Big ones."

Julia straightens. He ducks to tighten his overshoes, showing her with his posture that this is meant to be a secret.

It's not like Rafael to gossip. He's a good worker. A hard worker. Julia pretends to adjust her pant cuffs. "There's nothing left to cut." She requisitioned new gloves two years ago and is still waiting for them. Her right pointer finger slides out through taped-over repairs and the skin is permanently red.

"Angel, in the office? He says they're cutting the salary budget in half." Rafael's voice gets quieter until "half" is only mouthed.

Pedro presses his face between them. "Passing notes? I'll be at the top before you're done."

Rafael turns to taunt Pedro, and that's the end of the strange conversation. People are filing out of the room. The day has begun.

The catwalk rattles with feet as Julia jogs. The calls of "ready" start coming in on her radio before Julia has gotten to her section and clipped her belt to the safety line. It's a brave job, and they treat it as such. Every sunset they race to the top, for the privilege of turning the knob that starts the water flow and alerts the system washing is taking place. Julia has never been first, but she has been second.

She has never truly given her all. She has felt like she has, but there's a difference, between feeling it and doing it. She could, if she dug deep, run up the wall like her life depended on it. She could be first.

The sixteenth "ready" comes, and she leaps the first step, skittering mad and hard past the vertical. The city dome curves comfortingly under her gripping soles, and she sees the sun sinking in the west, painting oil slicks on the glass, the marks that never wash out, the bleeding minerals of the grilles.

This is her favorite part of the job, the beauty and solitude, the clouds rolling underneath the city, the sun melting into the soft horizon like a pat of butter in potatoes.

Her mother climbed cliffs on Earth with Julia's abuela. Her stories are peppered with references to anchor points and cracks and other things Julia doesn't know how to fit into her own experience of climbing. Once upon a time, her mother was here, lifting the beams supporting her into place. That is easier to imagine. The dome a fragile, empty thing, alone in the feral clouds of Venus, no city inside yet.

Julia can feel herself slowing near the top, arms and thighs getting lazy, pulling at her to slow down. She forces a second wind. The hard part is almost done.

Rafael is at the top already. She gives up, checks the hose and nozzle at her hip, turns the squeegee so it's at the angle she likes to grab it. She gets through the last few feet. The rest of the crew is coming into view. Rafael gets to turn the knob. Again. He does it like a stage magician revealing a dove.

The top of the dome is a sixteen-pointed star of time-painted titanium, and they, alone, get to enjoy it up close, to be out here with room to stretch. So they do, as they prepare to descend.

Pedro huffs. "I'm tired already."

He's just mad not to have made it to the top first. "If you want to quit, I'll take your pay." Julia tries not to sound out of breath. Pedro flips her off. No one's going to quit and lose their housing allotment.

She plays out a few feet of hose and hops back lightly. She hears Rafael teasing Pedro as she sprays a thin stream of soapy water along the rails that separate her section from the others. She's proud of her skill at this. She has the best water conservation scores.

She imagines the wash soothes the tired city. Acids eat every weak spot and lingers in unexpected salts. Without their careful maintenance, the dome could leak, and leaking meant sinking into the hellish pressure below. The air they breathe is also the lifting gas that holds the city aloft in Venus' denser atmosphere. Their parents' generation built a city to float in the clouds. Her generation keeps it flying.

She spots a nick and easily switches hands, holstering her water sprayer and pulling out the repair gel. Squirt, squeegee, and the white silica gel rapidly sinks into transparency as she switches hands again.

Hop back, spray, swipe clean. She gets into the rhythm, working left to right, then right to left as her section widens. She and Rafael meet at their boundary, and he looks over at her. "Have you thought about it? About what you'll do?"

Julia scowls. There's no time in her rhythm to respond, and she feels put upon that he throws troubles into her mind as she plays her rope out and drops out, down, left to start the next pass. There's Rafael coming toward her again. She has three hops and as many seconds to form a response. "So?" is all she comes up with.

"We need to stand together," he says. "All or none." And he's gone.

He thinks they'll be laid off? The city needs them. They never got a robot washer to work. Even if they did, there's no room in the city to store a washing robot, and to leave it out in the atmosphere is to ask for it to be slowly destroyed.

But he's serious.

What if they cut the staff? No. That would be too cruel with the housing rules. But they might. Would they move to washing every other sunset? Or will they each wash two sections? Her thighs burn as she hops. Her mother will hate that. Too much time in menial work, no time to improve herself.

"Why did you settle for this job where they can ask you to do this?" her mother will say.

The next time their paths touch, Julia and Rafael meet without words. It takes six hours to wash the dome now. Could she do this for twelve hours straight?

Her mother tells a story about climbing a limestone spire in El Potrero Chico, something like six hundred meters, with no guide rope. She never says how long it took, but that she lagged behind Abuela by hours.

Abuela exists in her mother's stories like a cartoon character or saint Julia doesn't quite believe in. Is this mythic grandmother meant to reflect on their relationship? Is there a moral behind the story she is expected to decipher? Did daughters always end up not quite as strong as their mothers?

Julia's left knee twinges when she plants to begin her next pass. An old injury, telling the tale of years on the job. Her mother wanted her to

work with her brain. "I busted my ass so you don't have to bust yours."
But it isn't any easier, busting her brain. The hardest problem in school
isn't a differential equation or history fact, it's finding a job you'll love
to do that wants you.

Rafael is hidden by the curve of the dome most of the time now. These
longer passes are grueling. Her shoulders strain without the break of
dropping to the next level. It's lonelier. The race and thrill are over. But
this is her work, and she is good at it, and she wants to keep doing it.

She side-hops over an apartment block. It's fascinating how people
take the same room and make it their own. A toddler looks out at her,
mouth open, pounding a doll's head with a plastic cube.

When she reaches Rafael again, she says, "All or none. Of course."

He gives her a sad look. "You promise? If they lay off, we all walk?"

She nods curtly. It's a drop and another long pass. The apartment
below has curtains drawn. A waxy white fabric, edges of burgundy that
must be the color on the inside. A spiderwort pokes its tendrils under
and around. Her mother is a terrible gardener but keeps trying. They
have a duty to grow green things. Every apartment a vegetable garden.

She only thinks of her mother in motion. Repotting, watering, tearing
up failures. Or pointing up at some girder or crossbeam to lecture about
bracing and counterbalancing. "Physics. That's everything, mija. Study
your physics and be a scientist and support me in my old age, eh?"

Would her mother understand if she walked off the job? Julia doesn't
know, but she feels strong, excited at the idea of doing something radical.

At the bottom of the window, Julia sets her feet on the lip of the city
and walks across. Her section is a fifteen-minute walk at the bottom,
when it was a single bound side-to-side at top. Her last pass is done
crouching and is the slowest pass of all. A trough under the catwalk
catches the soapy water, funnels it down to be filtered and processed.
She'll follow the pipes down, under the floor of the city. There, the rest
of the work shift will be cleaning and stowing the equipment. She tugs
her hose to start it retracting.

The weariness in her thighs and shoulders feels like a job well done.
She walks clockwise back to the airlock. Rafael's steps echo behind her.
She wants to look back, now that they are coconspirators, but doesn't.
She wants the dreary part of the night done, the indoor's grime and
machines. She'll get a beer before heading home. It's a gorgeous evening,
no higher clouds. The central square will be flooded with starlight as
second Sun Day ends and first Dark Day begins, the city speeding far
above the lagging ground in the atmospheric current. Forever the same.

It's possible Rafael is wrong. Maybe nothing will happen.

Angel, the office manager, is waiting in the locker room. That's not normal. He fidgets like he has to go to the bathroom while they take off their outdoor suits and hang their face shields. Rafael gives her a look that says, "I told you so."

Julia wishes she'd worn a better shirt today. This one has a stain on the sleeve where she set her elbow in spilled coffee. The face shields get rinsed in the sink and hung to dry. The suits go into a laundry hamper. The shoes rest in a tray full of acid-neutralizing chalk. She changes her socks. Many of the others don't, but she can't imagine going through the rest of her day in damp socks. Everyone is finished. Julia sucks the acid burn on the side of her pointer finger. One of the women starts brushing her hair. They should be going into the machine room now, but Angel is in the way.

He clears his throat. "The boss gave me the job of telling you guys. They're letting most of you go. We're keeping Rodriguez, Hammerstein, Corredor, and Lopez. I'm sorry."

Julia is Lopez. She feels a relief that squashes into instant horror and guilt. No one is talking, no one is moving. Rafael (Rodriguez) steps forward, shoulders wide. Is this it? Is he going to do something? Julia fears confrontations. She wants to hide. But she'll stand with him. She said she would.

Rafael asks, "How are four people expected to clean the whole dome?"

Angel's response sounds prepared. "You'll work four shifts, do it in sections. If we really stay on top of it, admin thinks it'll be enough. They're downsizing the office staff, too. Hector and Alverez from maintenance are going to do all the interior work. All you have to worry about are the windows."

"Fucking thanks." Marta Hammerstein throws a towel into her locker.

Pedro looks at Julia with hate in his eyes, and she realizes she isn't going to get a beer tonight, after all.

Rafael doesn't do anything. His face is trembling like he might cry or shout, but he doesn't say anything.

What's worse, neither does Julia.

Angel twists, half a shrug, half an aborted apology, and leaves.

Four shifts. Her mother will hardly see her. The argument between them is fully in her mind, as though it has already happened. She chose to be a dumb beast, not a knowledge worker. She can't afford to stand up for herself, when her mother . . . her mother built the city.

Normally, she would work a twelve-hour shift, with the interior work after the washing. They worked long on First Dark Day, got Second

Dark Day off, and did an inspection pass on First Sun Day, making small repairs, and got Second Sun Day off. It was a good schedule, a familiar rhythm. The document Angel sent to her drew out a complicated schedule that creeped forward and wrapped around the week, rather than working with it. Did they no longer care about the increased evaporation during Sun Days?

Julia walks half-blind, reading the schedule, dragging it over her old schedule, trying to make sense of it. No matter how slow she walks, she'll be home early. Behind her, Pedro is inconsolable, moaning and crying while another worker, RiRi, who has a strident voice, attempts to soothe him by pouring gasoline on his flame. "You know it's the corps. They're paying cash on the head for anyone we deport. You know why, don't you? Because their own workers are dying like flies. Like flies!"

She's almost home.

Julia lives in a frame stack building, aluminum beams white with age holding corrugated plastic in faded fruit juice colors. It sits wedged between newer buildings built on what had been streets, walkways relegated to tunnels underneath them, and even those are lined with sleeping bags. Their proud city resembles nothing so much as a warren of stacked plastic crates and abandoned campsites.

"They can't," Pedro moans. "They're not gonna . . . there's time, right? They gotta give people time."

"Time is an illusion." RiRi's getting louder. "They make you think you have time, but who's hiring, eh? Who's hiring?!"

A figure wrapped in a blanket rolls over, tightens the fabric around its head, and Julia flushes with embarrassment. How ungrateful they must sound, clean and well-fed, on their way to homes.

This isn't the utopia the Mexican government imagined, but they didn't know there would be refugees from the corporate factory-aerostats. Couldn't have dreamed such places would exist, so awful their workers were willing to risk the crushing depths to hop on a homemade glider or balloon and make it to the free air of New Tenochtitlan.

A door bangs open, a man shouts, private tragedy spilling into the street like food waste. Julia assumes it has nothing to do with her and studiously avoids looking until the man in the too-loose shirt is charging her way, and past her, and slapping Pedro.

"Pops! Ow!"

"You lost your job? You LOST YOUR JOB?"

Julia lowers her head and hurries, pretending that she doesn't hear every word.

"What are we supposed to do? Eh? What is your mother going to do when you get stolen away?!"

She pretends she isn't relieved by the contrast to her imagined argument with her mother. She hasn't lost her job. She will, at first, simply not mention the layoffs.

Julia's mother's apartment is small, smaller than the ones under Julia's section of dome. What had been "her" section. She supposes she'll now do a full quarter of the city. She's exhausted thinking about it. Like her first week on the job, when every night her body was spent and every morning her muscles felt like poorly set concrete.

Her mother bursts into the room the second she arrives, a tiny tornado with a gray buzz cut. "Are you okay? Did anyone get violent?"

Julia lets her mother drag her to the sofa and fuss over her. "You found out?"

"Eduardo. His daughter works in administration, and her wife is the facility manager's cousin. She says it's coming from the top. RyelCorp offered to pay for deportations in one big swoop, so the city wants all the unemployed people they can get at once."

"Ma, that's a conspiracy theory."

She shrugs. "I'm a lazy retired lady now, we do nothing but gossip."

Around the room, her mother's plants, quilts, and exercise equipment tell a different story. When will the concern fade and the recriminations start? "I guess I'll see how it works next sundown. The revised schedule."

Her mother freezes. "You didn't quit?"

She feels she has failed an important test. She also feels the threat of deportation to RyelCorp's factory bubbles. "Whatever the city needs, right?"

Her mother shifts on the sofa to face her directly, hands on her shoulders. "You listen to me, mija. Yes, those are words I've said, and I mean them most of the time, but not now." Julia's heart swells with love. "A city without people is only a ruin." Yes, that's it, exactly. But then her mother gives her a little shake and breaks her heart. "This is your chance. To leave that drudgery behind and get a real job."

Julia is on her feet so fast her mother's hands fly up as if in surrender. There's only the one bedroom. Julia sleeps on the sofa. She goes to the bathroom. At least it has a door.

The flimsy printed door doesn't muffle her mother's voice. "I shouldn't have said 'real.' I meant 'better.' When God closes a door, he opens a window."

Julia sits on the toilet and wishes there was a window she could escape through.

There are only four window washers now, and the city will not survive without their labor. It should be easy to band together, to refuse.

They have a group chat.

Marta: I'm pissed, too, but I can't afford to lose this job.

Corredor: TO ANY EXECUTIVE READING - I AM NOT A PART OF THIS DISCUSSION

Marta: Luis has a point. We'll get fired if they see this thread.

Rafael: But if we band together, they'd have to fire all of us.

Marta: You think they fucking won't?

That killed the thread. There was nothing after it but Rafael repeating some variation of the same thought:

Rafael: Come on, guys. I can't do anything on my own.

It's hot in the square, already halfway into the forty-eight-hour day. First Sun Day evening, or noon, as the sky tells it. The sun winks through the windowpanes, the heavy plants perspire. It smells both human and jungle. Here, the packing crate apartment buildings are a backdrop behind monuments and trees. The administration offices are built like a stepped pyramid, with lush foliage on every step.

Julia's mother is dragging her forward with a sweaty hand clamped manacle-tight on her wrist. Like she's a child again.

Julia looks yearningly toward the Cloud Bar's blue curlicue entrance. "Ma, this isn't going to do anything. You aren't important anymore."

"I should wash your mouth. I built this city. Now you'll see. It's not what you know all the time, sometimes it's who you know." She marches up to the reception desk at City Hall and knocks on it. "Hello, young man. We need to talk to Valeria, right away. Tell her it's Hortensia Lopez."

The man at the reception desk looks past them like they aren't there. Julia should have put on better clothes. She should have insisted her mother change. Their coveralls are like camouflage. They may as well be potted plants.

Hortensia continues speaking anyway. "The city is making a dangerous mistake. I won't have our maintenance workers mistreated this way. They keep us safe. When I—"

A woman in light, flowing shorts favored by the fashionable walks in, and the receptionist's attention immediately centers on her. Julia watches her mother's frown deepen as the man leans around her like she's an inconvenient post.

Hortensia says, "Did your mother not teach you respect? I'm here to see the mayor. It's Hortensia Lopez. She'll know me."

The receptionist draws back. "Do you have an appointment?" he asks, clearly assuming not. Assuming correctly, which is worse. "I can't even call her if you don't have an appointment. Try the public comments box."

Julia tries to get her mother to leave, but Hortensia has seen someone she knows and is marching across the foyer. "Darrin! Darrin Ruiz do not turn away from me, you know who I am!"

Her mother chases this man to a side entrance, where he turns at last and stares coldly. "Do you have a reason to be here?"

"Yes! My daughter, Julia, she has—"

"You don't belong here. Please leave." He walks away.

Hortensia blinks like she can't see. Julia wraps her arms around her bicep and urges her toward the exit.

"I held him at his first birthday party," Hortensia says.

As the sun sets, Julia prepares for work. She's gotten notice of the length of her shift, sixteen hours. Enough time to do three sections with three twenty-minute breaks between. Sixteen hours of washing. She packs muscle balm and an extra bottle of electrolyte-bearing water.

Her mother cracks the bedroom door, disarranged for sleep. "Mija what are you doing up so late?"

"I have to get to work. Double shift." She feels like a shady politician, prettying up the truth.

Hortensia's face falls in disappointment.

Julia keeps her eyes on packing her lunch box.

Her mother tries to grab her hand. She tries to evade her, but then Hortensia takes both hands, hers moist and warm from bed, like bread loaves ready to bake. "Don't go. They'll give you two weeks, it's plenty of time."

Julia doesn't want to go to work. She wants to be strong enough to say no. She wants to not feel this weight of expectation, the thousands of mornings of going to school, of going to practice, of going to work.

She flees the weight, and her mother's big, heavy hands. She goes to work.

Angel is in the locker room. It doesn't feel too small this morning. Marta is shaking her shoes out over the lime dust. Rafael doesn't look up from sealing his coveralls. Luis dresses like he's alone in the room.

Angel watches the four of them like they might bolt at any moment. "You made the right decision," he says to her.

Julia wonders when she made the decision. She goes to her locker. Someone has put gloves on top of hers, some other worker's less-worn pair. Pedro's? It feels wrong to be so close to Rafael when now there are many empty lockers. She starts to move her spare socks to the next locker over, and stops, seeing the name still there.

She turns to Rafael, waits for him to look at her. He doesn't. "Are we really doing this?" she asks him.

"Aren't we?" He sounds defeated.

She doesn't want to be on the side of defeat. She doesn't want to be on the side of Angel's untrusting smile. She feels, suddenly, disgusted at all of them.

She picks up her spare socks and snatches the photo of her ex-boyfriend and the picture from the New Year's Party. That's all that's hers in the locker. She turns and walks out.

The shaking starts before she passes Angel. Her anger cools to fear. Will they let her keep walking? She could be going to get something she forgot. Now she's at the exit. Now she's in the corridor. She realizes she's crumpled her photos.

"Lopez!" Angel reaches for her arm. She whirls on him, and he backs off, both hands in the air. Did she do that? With a look? "We picked you because you were the four best. Doesn't that mean anything? We picked you."

No one else has followed her out of the locker room. Not Rafael, not Marta. She feels defeat like a thing just under her stomach, waiting to rise. But Angel called her by her last name. The name that saved the city.

He says, "They'll just hire back one of the others, someone worse. The city will suffer."

Julia raises her chin. "That's their mistake to make."

She hates that she is doing what her mother wanted. When she gets home, her mother rises from the kitchen table, beaming joyful relief. Julia wants to scream, or argue, or explain, but instead she shakes and cries in her mother's arms. Hortensia rubs circles into her back. "No. It's good. You couldn't know your strength until it was tested."

Julia spends First Dark Day checking messages. The company gives her a second chance, twenty-four hours to return. She can use a sick day. They don't say who worked her shift, or if the dome went one-quarter unwashed.

Rafael wants to know if she hates him.

She doesn't, but she hates him asking.

At least he has finally done one thing: he has added all the laid off workers to the group chat.

Rafael: They're going to ask one of you to take Julia's place. Don't do it. Not unless they agree to hire more back.

Pedro: You're still working, right? Did you demand they hire us back?

Rafael doesn't answer. Julia wonders if she has been silent too long. She had something she could have said, once.

Hortensia cooks her best, most comforting dish, the cheese potato mash, and they finish off the red wine. It's almost a party, except for her mother going over the budget and writing out timelines they can live on. "There, you see? The charges for not having an employment voucher aren't so much. There is air, and water, and sewage. We can cover you two months."

"They deport after two weeks."

"I'm sure that's not really true. And I bet it doesn't take so long, now you're really looking. If you must, you'll find something temporary before two weeks are up."

Julia hasn't found any open positions she can apply to. She hadn't found anything in all the years she tried to meet her mother's expectations, and those years felt full of opportunity, the city uncrowded.

Her mother isn't worried, with her pension guaranteeing her residence until death. Julia tries not to resent that.

When Hortensia catches Julia going over the figures, she closes the screen. "But that's tomorrow and tomorrow, darling. Don't worry. I am the mother. I will tell you when to worry."

Sleeping in doesn't feel as good the second time. It's Sun Day and the light is strong, seeping through the cracks in the walls. Julia dresses in her best clothes and goes for a walk.

Her feet take her to work. They don't know any other walk.

She slows as the "employees only" sign comes into sight. She wonders who replaced her. How it felt, washing four sections instead of one. If the city will survive, or if the tired metal is even now being irrevocably eaten away.

A policeman stands at the door. Julia is several feet back, so she's surprised when he approaches. "You can't be here."

"I was just—"

"Leave or you'll be arrested."

Julia stares at him. "Arrested for what? This is a public corridor."

Which is how she gets arrested.

The jail is crowded. Each cell, designed to hold one person, holds five. One of the persons in her cell has peed on himself. The others huddle away from him, near the front. Their sweat and breath mingle in a moist fug.

She wishes she had her com so she could check the news. She wishes she'd done something more meaningful to get arrested than stand there.

The door to the corridor opens and a few people start shouting. When's my court date? Where's dinner? But the guard ignores them, leading her mother, who looks like she is claiming a prize at the end of this stinking corridor.

Julia is genuinely stunned her mother is getting her out. As she leaves the cell, she whispers, "Was it the mayor? Did you—?"

Her mother pins her a furious glance for one heartbeat.

She doesn't explain the bail until they are in their own apartment. Their savings, halved. The resources to find a new job shortened. "But it's fine. A mother provides. You'll find something."

They orbit each other in the cramped apartment like two positively charged magnets. They have three months of rent. Two months, if they want to eat.

Julia receives two messages. One from the city, stating that she has two weeks to find employment, or prove she is in a training program for employment, or she will be deported. She doesn't forward it to her mother, doesn't say "I told you so." The other message is from Angel, asking her to please come back, they will look the other way, just this once.

The group chat hasn't gotten any better.

Marta: They hired some untrained cloud-hopper. I blame you, Lopez! I'd take any of you fuckers over him. Smith's section may as well not get done. Found two cavities today, and it's only going to get worse.

Julia closes the feed. "I have an interview," she says, and keeps her head turned away from the way her mother brightens. She shouldn't have said it. She doesn't need an excuse to go outside.

The woman who has been sleeping on the edge of the walkway all week is gone, with her blanket and her bag of belongings. Julia wonders about tragedies that touch her life and don't. She'll never know where the woman came from, where she went.

Head down, she walks to the bar. It's been a long time since the after-work beer she never got, and she wants it. Deserves it.

Cloud Bar is beautiful. The floor is glass, and the ceiling, too, though nearby buildings block most of that view. The ceiling supports are covered in cotton fluff and sheer curtains to make it feel like you are in the sky. She has always loved this place. The prices are cheap before happy hour. She gets her favorite beer and finds a seat near the wall. Through the floor she can see the under-city and the RyelCorp High Pressure Lab, dangling like a rudder into the clouds. It was supposed to bring great, wonderful things to the city. It brought chemical engineers who got all the best housing, didn't pay taxes, and probably voted for the citizenship-by-employment mandate.

She imagines she can kick it off the city with her foot.

If she can't find another job in two weeks, she'll have to take Angel's offer. It feels like giving too much up, like admitting the administration can do this.

She sees Rafael arrive. Sees him see her and freeze. He looks to the exit. He sags. He comes to her, standing awkwardly like a new waiter. "I saw you got arrested."

"For walking on the sidewalk." She means it as half a joke; it comes out hard. Rafael looks like she kicked him in the gut. She shakes her head, loosening her hair and her tone. "The funny thing is, I wasn't even trying to picket or anything. I'd just come back to look at the place."

"Assholes!" He hovers. "Can I? I mean . . . "

"Sit. Don't explain or excuse, though. None of that."

He doesn't understand how much she means it because as he settles into the seat next to her, he explains himself. "I got scared. More scared than I thought I could get. I was ready to do it. Walk right out of there. I pictured every step, but then this thought popped into my head: what about my son? What about all the things he needs? You're single. You don't know what the burden feels like."

Julia considers dumping her beer on his head, but she doesn't think she can afford another. "What about when your son gets a job? What about when he's asked to work sixteen hours in the acid rain?"

"I didn't say I was right. I said I was scared." He waves for the bartender, who ignores him. "Anyway, I'm not going back." He pauses. She doesn't give him the reaction he's clearly pressing for. He slumps. "It was killing me, my hands, my legs. And yesterday, Marta slipped. Not a little slip, I mean she was hanging from her safety line, unable to get her feet under her until me and José got to her. And my legs were shaking so I almost couldn't help. It terrified me. What if we all had slipped? No paycheck is worth dying for." He holds up two fingers and exchanges nods with a waiter. He looks back at Julia. "You don't believe me? You think I'm too strong to collapse? Girl, I only ever beat you by a step, you realize that?"

"No, I believe you." She avoids looking at him. "About being tired." Had she gotten the offer to return only because Rafael quit? "You're one of the good ones," the message said, "You care about the city." It implies there are "bad ones."

Rafael fidgets. "I mean it about not going back. I threw all my gear in a bundle off the platform! I made sure I couldn't chicken out again. Ah, bless it." This he says to the beer approaching their table. "It'll be my last foolish act. They've outlawed striking. I only got out by saying I wasn't doing that, I was quitting. So that's it." He looks into his beer as though seeing the end of something. "I checked with RyelCorp, they aren't hiring. I thought maybe your mother has some connections with the building crews? I'll do anything."

Julia imagines the sunrise on top of the dome, who will see it. She drains her beer. It hits her hard. Not enough to eat, lately. She doesn't want to feel guilty. She stares past Rafael, at the community news report. The high school baseball finals. Kids smiling against the projected green field, swinging real bats at holographic balls and running on treadmills. It's hard to see it the way the kids will.

"They got Pedro," Rafael says and cringes like he wants to take it back. He lowers his voice. "I mean, he's gone. There was a shipment to the corp domes yesterday. His folks aren't talking."

The news report flashes red. Emergency. "Low Pressure Detected in Section 4." The steady buzz of talk and motion around the room freezes into one tense silence, all eyes fixed to the man who appears on the screen. "There is no cause for panic. A leak has been detected, but balloons are being deployed. Citizens are recommended to seal their rooms if they can be sealed. This is only a precaution."

Some people leave. Some go back to their drinks. The general buzz of conversation shifts, becomes serious. Julia wants to spit acid, call out the greed that so predictably led here. What would she say, though, who would listen?

The news shifts to a shot of the cleaning crew—her cleaning crew, leaving work. It must have been shot weeks ago. "The blame for the dome leak is being laid on workers who walked off the job in a bid for shorter working hours."

Julia feels a pulse of anger so visceral it's like a fireball expanding from her chest. Someone shoots her a dirty look. A familiar face. A regular. Does he recognize her from that split second of video?

Julia stands up. "You want something to do? Come on, let's go."

Rafael's face is slack with shock, but he obligingly stands. "Where are we going?"

"To get arrested."

• • •

There are three police officers at the turn for the maintenance employee entrance. As Julia and Rafael approach, they straighten from lounging against walls, set their feet wide. A violent intention thrums through their posture.

"This is where we walk on the sidewalk?" Rafael whispers, his voice wavering.

Julia strides forward. "We're here to fix the leak." It comes out more confident than she thought she could sound. A clarion call, a command. One of the cops steps back.

Only one.

She turns to Rafael. "Come on." He nods, solemn.

They make it even with the police, not half a step further, and hard hands are on her biceps. She and Rafael are pushed back. One officer, a woman, says, "Get out of here. Try that again, and we'll have to take you in."

Julia almost laughs. "Why not take me in now?"

The cops look at each other. Julia has a guess. That jail was pretty full before. Has someone said not to bring more people in? She hooks Rafael's arm and leads him away.

Julia makes her first post to the group chat.

Julia: Who's up for storming the locker room?

Rafael: Julia wants to break in, help fix the dome. It'll show the city we're the right side. There are only three guards, and they're not very threatening. Just kinda scowled at us.

No one posts "yes," though there are a number of icon responses. Eyeballs. A fist. Rafael posts a date and time. Julia has no idea what to expect when it arrives.

On the corner with the noodle place, they meet RiRi and Rafael's former roommate and a friend of a friend who used to date Pedro. The roommate had worked on windows once, in high school, but the ex is just there for moral support and muscle. Julia feels like she has misjudged each of these people by not recognizing their compassion before now. She wants to cry, and to hug them. Instead, she just nods.

They form two rows, two and three, and they march right past the guards. The police grab her, again, but Julia punches her fist into the air, pushing the hold up her arm. She presses forward, through hands and a tripping leg, and the door is in front of her.

Someone grabs her hair, then, and yanks her off her feet.

It's a mess. A tangle of limbs and shouting. It feels more like children wrestling than something adult. There's a sharp smell of ozone, and Rafael cries out.

It ends quickly after the taser.

Julia gets a fat lip and zip ties on her wrists. The five of them are sat down in a row, Rafael shaking his head and blinking like he can dispel the memory of electricity.

One cop paces back and forth in front of them, his fists tightening and releasing as if he doesn't know what to do with the energy. The other two confer, anxious whispers that get loud enough to hear. "So call." "I'm not going to—" "Look."

Two more police officers arrive. One has the golden eagle of a commander. She stops three feet away and holds up a hand. "I am very disappointed in you," she says to Julia and her companions. "We're in a dangerous situation and the city needs you to be calm, to not make matters worse."

RiRi snaps, "We were trying to—" and is kicked by the officer who had been pacing.

"Now," the commander says, a gentle admonishment, as if this were a child drawing on the walls. "None of that. We need to be civilized." She hooks her thumbs on her belt. "The jail's a bit crowded at present, so I'm going to let you off with probation. Don't mistake this for nothing. You're out of warnings. If you so much as spit on a walkway, your asses are going straight to deportation holding. Is that clear?"

Are they supposed to answer? Agree to this? Pedro's ex murmurs "Yes, ma'am," and the others follow. The woman stares at Julia until she ducks her head and says, "Yes, ma'am," too.

They reconvene on the High Path, a narrow public walkway that loops through the upper levels of the city, connecting to buildings and support struts, with a few benches and baskets of plants attached to its sides. None of them have the money to waste on beer or even hot noodles. Julia feels like she's in a trap and only waiting for it to snap shut. There's still a red line on her wrist from the zip tie.

RiRi sighs and sticks their legs over the edge to dangle. "I think it's that prisoners can't be deported before trial. That's why they don't want to arrest us. This is actually worse, this one-offense warning."

Rafael is unfairly happy, pacing back and forth, making the walk bounce with his steps. "No. This was a step. A stride. They backed down. We have them. Five people is too many for them to arrest. Imagine what we can do with this!"

"Get beat up again?" Pedro's ex asks.

They can see so much from up here. Part of a mural that might be a child throwing a baseball or just reaching for a glowing, floating one.

The odd, organic blue plastic of the university annex peeking around the traditional, square shapes of other buildings. Graffiti. There's a man leaning on a railing below them, gesturing now and again as he talks to someone remotely. His forearms are like drumsticks. A woman waters a sweet pea vine in a window to the right of him.

Walkways and stairways and floors, all built one atop another, atop empty air. Julia imagines it falling, emptying, ending. She imagines what it was like when her mother first saw it, when there was just an aerostat and a gantry and a fabber spinning out material from clouds.

The others haven't stopped arguing. "Well, what are we supposed to do, then?" Rafael demands. "Nothing?"

Julia can see through crossed walkways and power lines to workers brushing a mylar sheet against the interior of the dome. An ugly, temporary fix. It brings the anger back.

Two men are jogging on the walkway. Rafael and Pedro's ex have to squeeze to the side to let them pass. As they do, one of the joggers mutters, "Lazy bums."

The other is louder. "If you don't love the city, leave it."

The first whispers something to him, and they both turn back, scowling, and it's not the casual hatred of the rich for the poor, it's specific. They know who they are looking at, and they want very much to push the lot of them off the walkway.

Julia gets up and goes toward the nearest stairs down.

She didn't expect Rafael and RiRi to come with. They followed her down and pestered until the direction she walked made it pointless to hide her destination. "I'm going to talk to Angel." She showed them the message, that she could still have her job back.

"Are you, though?"

Julia shrugs. "It'll get me in to talk to him."

Angel holds the door frame as if to prevent them from entering the administrative office. "Are you ALL expecting me to give your jobs back?" He looks pointedly at Rafael.

"We just want to talk," Julia says.

Angel starts to close the door. Julia pushes her arm into the gap. "You *know* the dome needs regular maintenance. You know it's more work than four people can do."

"It's not my decision."

"Then let us talk to whoever's it is."

Angel shakes his head. "I need to keep my job."

His exhausted expression isn't different from Marta's when she said the same thing. "Do you? Why? Who decided we had to bow to jobs? What about my mother? What's her job?"

"She served the city."

"So did I."

Angel presses his hands together. "Please. Just take the job back. They're already threatening to ship you off for leaving."

Julia has nothing to threaten other than violence, and she doesn't want that. Angel is awful, but he is also a person. "Let us cut through the office."

He frowns. "What? No. I just said. I need this job!"

Julia puts her hand on Angel's chest and pushes. She increases force until it's enough and he stumbles back. She pushes him all the way to his desk, and his arms pinwheel until they clasp the front edge. "So we forced our way in," she says, and leaves him there, walking to the inner door, the one that leads from administration to operations, and from there, to the locker room.

She still doesn't expect Rafael and RiRi to follow, but they do.

She doesn't go deeper into operations looking for the boss. She doesn't think it would help. There's an endless line above Angel, of people just doing their jobs, pointing up until you got to the top, and the top person points down at the bottom, saying, "I need to keep their support."

The locker room is a tumbled mess. Anti-acid powder footprints track everywhere. Julia finds a clean pair of grip-soles and puts them on over her regular shoes. If she's doing this, she might as well be comfortable.

RiRi hangs by the door, uncertain, but Rafael starts gearing up, taking gloves from this locker, a face shield from that. RiRi shakes their head. "So, you're . . . breaking in here, just to work?"

"Someone has to do this." Julia hasn't thought too much beyond that. She's angry and tired of being blamed for not doing a job she wants to do.

Rafael settles the shoulder straps of a safety harness and grins. "It's perfect. We save the city, we show them what side they should support."

Not much Rafael has said has ever turned out true, but Julia wants to take comfort in his optimism. She starts to put on a face shield, finds it stinks of garlic and sickness, and puts it back, picking up another.

That's when the door bursts open. She doesn't hear what they shout, something like "get down" or "hands up"—it's a percussion note, like the boots, the batons hitting the lockers. The police fan in quickly, one left, one right, one left.

RiRi stumbles, pushed down by them. They look up, disbelief in their eyes, their arms cradling their head, and then RiRi is diving toward the police, rolling on the floor into their legs.

Rafael has already gone out the airlock. Julia hates that she doesn't hesitate longer.

Rafael slams the door behind them and twists the handle off. Julia doesn't think that will actually do anything, but there's no time to argue about it. She grabs her rope and starts climbing.

It's full Sun Day, not the right time for doing this, and the heat is unexpected, strange. The texture of her feet on the glass feels stickier.

Whatever's happening behind her, she is soon absorbed in the task of climbing. She's already out of shape, gasping more than usual. Or maybe it's the heat.

She skitters to the top to see Rafael a few paces behind her. Sees him see her and slow down, checking his squeegee on his hip. When they both reach the top, he bows to her, gesturing.

"Dork," she says, but she twists the knob. It doesn't feel how she'd imagined.

With gestures, they split the dome in two. They go slowly, no time limit, checking for damage. It doesn't take long to find the first crack. Julia smooths it and wonders if someone will climb up behind her, yank her off the city. There are emergency service balloons and helicopters. Her back prickles and not all the sweat is from the sun.

Two passes, and it's already feeling longer than doing the base of her old section. Her radio crackles. She forgot it was built into the helmet, that she was wearing it.

"Rafael Rodriguez. Julia Lopez. By order of the chief of police, you will not be permitted to reenter the city."

Julia stops where she is, the too-loud, hard voice echoing in her mind. She keeps expecting them to say more. She hears the rhythmic jingling of Rafael's harness as he hops to her. He's breathing heavy. "They're locking us out."

Julia readjusts her grip on the safety line. She looks at her feet. They're still on the flattish top of the dome, the view beneath her is a rooftop with skylights and vents. Will the acid rain melt their clothes first? No, she's being silly. They'll die of thirst long before anything else gets them.

Julia sees what might be a crack to her right. "See you on the other side," she says and goes to it.

Rafael is still and quiet a long time before he resumes washing.

Two more passes. They get another warning not to go near the airlocks. Rafael finds a discolored patch. "I don't know if anyone is listening on this channel. But it's grid 4-C-10. Someone should make a note and come back here."

Julia is exhausted. She finds Rafael has stopped, sitting, his knees up, on the curve of the glass. "We're not getting through this in four hours, chica. Take a load off."

So she copies his posture and looks out on the cloud sea. The tantalizing deep valleys that look like they hold secrets. The soft curving slopes she imagined sledding down as a child. "We're going to die here."

Rafael snorts like it's a joke. "And I'm already almost out of repair gel."

When their legs are rested, they resume their work. There doesn't seem to be anything else to do.

On the next pass, they are even with some apartments, and people have gathered to watch for them. A man with a baby waves. Julia waves back.

The next floor down, there are more people. They don't look angry at them. They look excited. It gives Julia strength. She works harder.

Then she sees her mother.

It's a rooftop park. A nicer neighborhood than theirs. She went there once with a school club, to do some plant-identification assignment. Julia can't see the little cards on the beds now because the rooftop is crowded with people holding signs.

"Maintenance is life," reads a large one. Another says, "Justice for workers."

She is startled by two girls waving at her, shaking a banner. "I stand with Lopez."

Her mother's sign is one of the nicest, of course, with clean, elegant letters. "My daughter has the most important job in the city."

ABOUT THE AUTHOR

Marie Vibbert has sold over eighty short stories to places like *Nature*, *F&SF*, and *Analog*. Her work has been translated into Vietnamese and Chinese. Her debut novel, *Galactic Hellcats*, about a female biker gang in outer space rescuing a gay prince, was on the British Science Fiction Association's long list for 2021. Her second novel, *The Gods Awoke* (Journey Press, September 2022), is about a powerful telepathic sentience discovering she is not a god.

Marsbodies

ADELE GARDNER

The Seven Minutes of Terror had never been so terrifying. Or exhilarating. We hurtled down, our heat shields roaring. In my capsule, despite being harnessed in, my Marsbody trembled in the relentless vibration that accompanied the sound of the inferno. I raced down at a thousand miles an hour. The supersonic parachute deployed with a nine-G jolt.

Right on schedule, the heat shield popped off. The disc soared off like a Frisbee. The pocked dunes of Mars zoomed in to giant size with frightening speed. (Two hundred miles an hour!) The backshell flew off, and I zoomed to one side, out of the way of the parachute array as the rocket brakes kicked in. Then the sky crane halted me, twenty meters above the surface.

I extended my wheels and swung down on the tether. I still had to fight human instincts that told me this was way too high. But my wheels touched down lightly. I checked myself, automatic, obsessive: no damage. My teammates and I checked in, their braying cheers filling my head with a warm hum as I rolled to meet them.

That was fun, ha. Have you ever had a robot party? We rolled around hooting and whistling our delight, waving extensor arms, and rotating our gyroscopes. We looked like the wacky children of the original Mars rovers, except with more of everything: arms, equipment, chambers for samples and processing.

Now, this was fun, but with twenty of us down here, all of us in fine working condition, we got right down to business. We only had a few hours before night fell, and the temperature dropped to minus one hundred and forty degrees Fahrenheit. Our Marsbodies could still operate, but we expended less energy when we didn't have to simultaneously provide our own heat and light.

As we set up the base, I sought out Jin Kyung Mi. My best friend. She looked like herself, as much as any of us could: the faceplate viewscreen perched atop her spindly body bore an image of the face I'd loved on Earth, filmed and broken down into its component emotions so that she could still communicate with us in this wordless human way. We worked side by side in harmony, like the longtime teammates we were.

Jin Kyung Mi and I had known each other since elementary school. Beautiful, thoughtful, artistic, quiet in a good way that meant she was thinking carefully and giving you the space to do so too, to enjoy the moment for whatever it might bring, even if—especially if—that was work. A richness that meant I knew that when I did speak, she would listen and take me seriously, and when she spoke, it would be something I would stop everything to hear, her mellifluous voice speaking to the heart of things, helping me see the world in new ways.

Of course, as we grew older, there were other things; her long, shining black hair, the way her deep brown, East Asian eyes crinkled when she smiled. When we were in fifth grade, she drew a lot of Korean princesses, and I secretly thought she might be one of them; her kindness was proof, a forgiving air that reminded me of the noblesse oblige in the Arthurian tales I was reading then.

Living so near the coast, we were lucky to have a wide mix of cultures in our community; our neighbors in the townhouse complex came from New York (my family), Saudi Arabia, Korea, Vietnam, Alabama, Nigeria, Germany, Puerto Rica, Japan, and South Africa, and those were just the kids we played with in our court. Many of us came from several places, like my own Irish-German-English-Pennsylvania Dutch mix, or Pamela's African American-Japanese. It was partly thanks to the military and the nearby base where Dad worked. We loved it.

But Jin Kyung Mi was my favorite, the special friend I sought above all others, who wouldn't laugh at me like my brothers when I asked her to help me make tiny plates and tables for my dollhouse out of the clay we dug from the hill behind our school. When I stopped by and knocked on her family's door—at a carefully chosen time when she'd let me know she'd be done with violin lessons, and her mother would let her come out to play—whenever she appeared on her stoop, at that first sight of my friend, my heart lifted with warmth like a hot air balloon. Anything was possible.

As you can tell, I loved Kyung Mi. I guess maybe it showed, though she never spoke of it. I heard the snickering, the way the other kids called me gay, then explained to me what it meant, not in the most flattering terms. We were only ten. But I did love her. Then, and ever since.

That's why, when she turned to science with an eye on the space program, I did, too. One of her several specialties (we needed at least three to be considered for the long-term Mars program) was robotics, while mine was the mapping of the human mind to a programmed simulation. We worked hard to hit every mark and then some; even then, it seemed women had to accomplish five times as much to be noticed and given an "equal" chance—but Kyung Mi was still so kind, giving time from her own limited sleep to assist newer astronaut candidates.

But Kyung Mi was straight. At least, so she told me, when we were undergraduates, and I finally got the nerve to ask her out. We were roommates, and she was crying over another jerk, so maybe it wasn't the best timing. But I wanted her to know she was loved. That, even though I knew she liked guys and I had no chance, there was one person whom she could count on, who'd take good care of her heart.

I swear my heart was going so fast I thought I might be having some kind of attack. "I love you, sweetheart. Don't worry. I love you." I stroked her shining black hair, smoothing it away from her tearstained face. "I know it's not the same for you. Believe me, I wish I was a man, and not just so we could be together. If you want me to move out, I understand. But I just want you to know you're so worthy of being loved. Don't let that jerk poison your mind. You're the best person I know."

I proceeded to tell her. All the while, my heart was in my throat, and I was sitting next to her, stroking her back where she huddled over the end of the couch.

At last the heavy gasps settled into long sighs. Kyung Mi sat up. I handed her tissues and sat back quietly while she composed herself. It wasn't easy. But I thought about the many times she'd been quiet for me, like after my mother died.

"I do love you, Peri. Please understand. I'll always love you. You're my best friend. But I'm not wired the same way you are. I don't want you to break your heart pining after me."

I admit, I had tears in my eyes, but I appreciated her honesty.

So I was surprised when she came to my bunk the night before we set off on our mission. "It's the last time we'll be human together for a while," she said. In that narrow bunk, her kind eyes and gentle hands assured me she wanted to be here. I showed her all the love I'd kept pent up, and she showed me how deep a well our friendship was. She didn't make any promises. She couldn't. We effectively wouldn't have bodies up there. And I knew better than to think beyond the joy of this moment. And so we slept at last.

The next morning, we entered hibernation. No going back until the mission was complete.

Twenty astronauts slept under the tender care of our robot pilot. Hibernating humans required less oxygen, food, water, and luggage—leaving room for yet more building blocks that could be sent to Mars. But oh, the dreams! I think I got about a lifetime of happiness with Kyung Mi on the months out.

Once our robot pilot achieved orbit, we roused a bit: just awake enough to connect with our Marsbodies. This was the trickiest part. Frankly, it was terrifying. We'd trained for months to stay calm, not to give in to the panic of suffocation in the goo as we transitioned from dreams to paralysis, to the absolute sense-D that preceded connection with our Marsbodies. Because we had to be awake to switch those pathways on.

The specially shielded hull and the goo itself kept us safe from radiation; automated processes would stimulate muscles and keep us sharp; but we didn't have the resources on board to maintain life support for the ten years we'd be out here, terraforming and building habitats in our hardy Marsbodies. We just had to trust that on board the ship, our computer would monitor human life signs and replenish the oxygen, nutrients, and life-giving elements of the goo. Because we couldn't sense those bodies. We wouldn't know if they began to rot.

For us, it had begun: life on Mars.

On days without dust storms, when we'd finished our tasks, Kyung Mi and I sat on a ridge, looking up at all the stars. They looked so very, very clear. The night chill deepened. We could feel it; our sensors fed into our brains. We hunkered near each other in the dark, draping extensible arms over one another's hulls for added stability. Our aerogel and heaters kept us warm, and our nearness cut the wind. I could feel the faint purr of the motors rumbling deep within Kyung Mi, a soothing vibration like my brother's cat Jimmy back home.

We'd return to the joint cabin. In order to cushion the mind from unrelenting toil and prevent soul-sapping ennui that might lead to mistakes or to overlooking solutions, we'd been encouraged to bring entertainment and make use of downtime.

Downtime could be weird in a Marsbody. It was the time you felt most out of yourself, disconnected, because you weren't focused on work; because on Earth, that might be the time you felt most aware of your physicality, your desire for mental or physical pleasures. It was a time when you were allowed, even encouraged to think of yourself, in a good way. Who you were. What you liked. Self-care. Who you wanted to spend time with.

We weren't eating on Mars, but I still had my comics and music, downloaded and stored in my Marsbody's long-term memory cache. I had movies and shows, too, and so did the others, and we swapped, we talked, we even watched things together. Sometimes the group chat veered into the pleasures we missed.

"What do you like on your pizza?" I asked. I had pizza on the brain—my favorite food.

"Anchovies," said Kyung Mi.

Benny wrinkled his nose. "God, I hate those things. How can you eat them?"

Kyung Mi shrugged. "I tried them once on a Hawaiian pizza. You know, pineapples, ham . . . anchovies. I fell in love."

"I'm falling a little in love myself," he said gallantly. I remembered Benny, how he'd looked on Earth, in his human form. That impish grin looked even funnier atop the dome of his robot body, an egg with eight skinny extensor legs that let him run like a spider. That goofy guy was just her type.

In private chat, Kyung Mi sent me a drawing she'd made of my human self wolfing down a pepperoni pizza and sharing some with Marsbody-me. I chuckled.

"I can't wait to get home," Sargon said. "No offense. You're all great, but I miss alone time. For one thing, it's really hard to concentrate on writing a novel. I just can't get a nice, good block of time to concentrate because everything you all say and do is so interesting, I can't pull myself away!"

Mara said, "All of us have things we want to do. But this is also probably the most exciting thing we'll do in our lives. Seriously, we're on Mars. We're robots, for goodness sake! Nothing else is going to measure up to this. Tell me I'm wrong!"

Of course, we could not.

Were we the robots? Or were we riding robots who had just a hint of sentience themselves? Were we brushing off on them? I knew a lot about encoding human personalities, but I couldn't always tell. It wasn't part of our mission, but I'd started keeping a private log.

It had started sometime after the second week, when Benny's robot body had saved him from an avalanche without any hint of being asked. Lots of other little hints of assistance; an extra push here, a head unconsciously turned toward an interesting scientific sample we hadn't noticed before there.

We talked about it sometimes in downtime. Always and only the positive aspects. After all, our robot-suits were listening.

We'd been there quite a while when we started speculating about what would happen when we left.

Serena said thoughtfully, "Leaving our Marsbodies is going to be like death."

"For them? Or for us?" I wondered.

"If they get other operators," Pinter said, "it'll be like reincarnation, only in reverse. Our children, maybe. It won't be us."

Benny said, whimsically, wistfully, "Do you think the robonauts will know the difference?

And Mara said quietly, "I think they will. They've got that primitive AI functionality that gives us an assist. They're going to be programmed with their upkeep, housekeeping tasks during the interval while no one's directing them. They're rather like our cats and dogs. Haven't you felt that? A kind of warm comfort and affection. They may not be fully sapient, but they are aware, and they care what happens to us. They'll have to go on without us, and they won't know why. Or is that just me?"

Quietly, Kyung Mi mused, "Dogsbodies."

"Do you mean them? Or us?"

Pinter laughed and said, "Well, we ought to go on and explore Pluto with them. Then the Dog Star."

Serena said with quiet certainty, "We will someday."

"Maybe so," I said slowly. But I was exploring the strange warmth I felt about my upper carapace, a comforting sensation that reminded me of when my brother's orange tabby cat draped my shoulders, purring. I could see Jimmy's sad eyes as he sat on my suitcase during my last visit, as if he'd been pleading with me not to go. The pang, like a rod through my chest: so long, so long since I'd seen my family. Would I ever see them again?

"I miss Jimmy too," Jin Kyung Mi said softly.

Kendra said, "I miss my dad. And my baby brother, Robert. He was only one when I left, and his head smelled really good." She laughed, using the carefully modulated robotic equivalent we'd all practiced to avoid blaring like scary monsters.

"Yes. Babies smell good. I wish—" Even a robot could hang its head.

Kyung Mi said, "Don't worry, Mara. One of the good things about this setup is our bodies are well cared for. We should be biologically younger than our technical ages when we get back."

"Because our bodies aren't lived in," Leonard said gloomily. Last week, he'd received a cold, clipped message from his wife. She was leaving him. Leonard's work began to suffer. None of us wanted to say anything to him about it, but I knew I wasn't the only one watching his increasingly erratic behavior with anxiety.

But it wasn't only Leonard whose health was deteriorating, mental or otherwise. The longer we humans stayed in our robot shells, the more problems developed. With such complex structures over such a length of time, this seemed inevitable. And some of it was just the wearing away at our patience of this increasingly interminable sojourn.

Last night I woke up during the erasure.

It was a glitch. It had never happened before.

In our Marsbodies, we only had so much onboard room to store our memories. The Marsbodies derived mission data, which had to be stored; but even with the planetside computer, not everything could be saved. Just think about the human process of sleep, during which the mind somehow decides what will become long-term memory, what is retained for temporary short-term, and what can be safely erased.

After downtime, each night we'd enter a sleep period, to facilitate the computer's version of this process.

I half-woke, which shouldn't have been possible in maintenance mode. I found my mind in the middle of singing the remnants of the song I'd spontaneously created the day before while we'd worked, which had been so catchy, and which I'd repeated enough times that I'd surely remember it. But now I couldn't remember all the words, just snippets. Most of the melody seemed intact, but without the words. I couldn't be sure.

I was still groggy, half-asleep, but as I often am in dreams, found myself cheerful in a way I seldom feel in real life when initially confronted by a challenge. Kyung Mi and I stayed up late last night reading comic books, so I didn't have enough time to sleep before work to record the song. But I went back to humming it over in my mind, groping for the missing words, hoping that this time I'd remember it, like an interesting dream—that I'd interrupted the destructive process of wiping the memory banks in time.

But no. When morning dawned, it was gone, despite that catchy rhythm.

I remember trying to save it. I remember it was a good song, which Kyung Mi seemed to enjoy. When I'd started singing, creating words and melody as I went, I'd been happy, in a deep, satisfying way I didn't want to question. It wasn't just the sheer pleasure of the amazing sequential art.

Each night, before I shut my unit down, Kyung Mi and I sat together, plugged in so our speech wouldn't disturb the others. I watched her smiling faceplate as we conversed. It sounds corny, but as we secured each other for sleep—running visual and diagnostic checks on one another like a grooming ritual—it felt like a sweetness I'd known only a few times on Earth. They might be faceplates with viewscreens, but it sure felt like staring into loving eyes, that unconditional bond, deep beyond words.

So it upset me—made me sad to part with any moment of that. I could feel the chomp, chomp, chomp as my brain ate away all those bits of ephemeral information. As I slept, I must have been unconsciously trying to save this song, humming it as I woke. But like so many dreams, I couldn't hang onto it. It was gone.

I could almost hear the echoes. Maybe if I pulled on the tail—maybe I'd saved just enough—

This was the panic that woke me in a cold sweat in my Marsbody, fighting to move. Fighting to think. Fighting to remember.

Don't wipe! I pleaded with my brain. *Not now, when she finally loves me!*

Desperately I repeated the song—the scraps I now remembered— hoping that even if my robot brain wiped things, maybe my meat brain might save it. If enough of my meat brain was engaged to know, and I wasn't just the autonomic ghost of a hibernating mind.

So the next day I found myself in an odd mood. I woke up with a sense of loss whose strength bewildered me, even though I remembered that frightening feeling of my brain being chomped. I know we were supposed to focus our attention on the scientific challenges of Mars, but I couldn't stop looking at Kyung Mi. Something seemed—off. Her graceful motions would stop in the middle, for just a millisecond. A burr in the joint, which maybe only I noticed. But it was another thing that shouldn't be happening.

The Martian sand got into everything. Maybe it got into her joints, in spite of all the insulation. But her calculations were off. A storm rose, and I couldn't seem to get her moving. It was strong enough, I needed to get her back to the tent quickly. She kept tripping. I hovered close, moving ahead to smooth the sand, reaching out a retractor arm to clear the path of stones.

We all made it into our mobile camp just as the horizon turned crimson with dust.

I was still settling Kyung Mi in a safe place in the back to examine her when Sargon and Kendra rumbled in, arguing, their face screens turned toward each other while their onboard guidance systems moved them forward. This made them clumsier than they needed to be, even with robot limbs. They collided and tripped Benny, who broke one of the struts. Kendra leaped forward, shooting out a telescoping arm to bind it in place and keep the roof above our heads. It drummed with debris. As I moved to help, I could feel the vibrations.

I returned to Kyung Mi. "How are you feeling?"

Her sleek eyestalks rotated in the "no" signal.

I grabbed the nearest sterilization kit and began to buff the dirt and crud from her joints. "Maybe you should go back upstairs." This was an option reserved for the direst circs, but I had a terrible feeling as I manipulated her limbs and felt only a weak, fluttering response. As if the human mind had only a tenuous grasp on the Marsbody's controls. I didn't want to say it, but if there was something wrong with her human body, there was no one upstairs to help her.

"If I do that, I might never get back into this body," Kyung Mi said calmly.

"Maybe I'll go, too." I used the buffing rag to smooth her dome. No one else was watching, so I mixed in a small amount of metallic polish and brought her faceplate up to a glossy shine. As I smoothed away the dust, the colors on Kyung Mi's face screen brightened, as if her mood were lifting. That gentle smile. I wanted to hug her. The impossibility of that felt like beating my head against a wall.

"Besides," she said, "if I can't get back into my Marsbody, there's not enough life support up there for the rest of the mission."

I stroked her shell. "What if we created a small containment area just big enough for you?"

"Still not enough."

"Those trees are doing well. I think we should be able to leave soon."

"No way," Sargon said. "If we don't maintain the dome, the first big storm will take them down."

Kendra argued, "The rock face will shield them. We set up for this. We bolstered that dome, and it's going to stand. If it doesn't none of us have a chance here anyway."

"Besides," Leonard added, "we wasted way too much air on that dome to let it blow down. That's our fallback position, so it had damn well better stay intact."

Kyung Mi could barely move. Slowly, she stretched out one extensible limb to adjust my faceplate, a pensive smile on her screen. But even her face kept breaking up with static. Was it just an unusual transmission disruption effect from the storm? Fighting back panic, I reviewed schematics and readouts and found nothing. Was the fault in her Marsbody? Or was her body on the ship injured? Dying? What about those domes? Some of the oak groves might almost be strong enough to support human life, at least for a few years, especially if it was just one person. Could we get her out of stasis and downstairs if we needed to?

By now, the team was involved. No more joking or fighting. Everyone knew there was something wrong with Kyung Mi. Kendra and Mara started checking on the nearest dome, while Sargon came over to help me run diagnostics on Kyung Mi. Benny and Serena kept pinging the ship for status updates. All they got back was the smiley-face, automated "Everything's under control."

"That could mean anything." Benny uttered a mournful whistle. In the emotion of the moment, we were forgetting our human mannerisms, letting the simpler robot gestures shine through. Over the years, this shorthand had made more and more sense as we got more comfortable with ourselves.

Leonard said glumly, "What if an asteroid hit the ship and wiped out the robot pilot? And us?"

Serena looked scared. "Peri? Is that possible?"

I really didn't want to talk about this. That experience, waking up while the computer chomped my memories, haunted me as I said, "It's possible."

Benny demanded, "If we're dead, who's running our Marsbodies?"

"We are."

"That makes no sense!"

Kyung Mi smiled up at me as I met all fourteen of her hands with mine, forming what we called a Perfect Union. I said, "If we were killed, our Marsbodies would still have our recorded personalities and memories. We did an elaborate fit of each person's mind, creating an impression in the robot brain so that we'd feel 'at home' in our own skulls."

"So these robots might be the only thing keeping us alive?" Sargon sounded incredulous.

"Let's not jump to conclusions," Kendra cautioned.

My mind was racing. Selfishly, I couldn't help thinking about the fact that back in our human bodies, the relationship between Kyung Mi and me might not even exist. But I said, "We need to get upstairs and see what's going on."

"You mean wake up?" Leonard looked at me sharply.

"In a manner of speaking."

"You want us to kill ourselves," Benny said, rolling around us and back and forth in a frantic, haphazard way.

"No, I want us to save Kyung Mi."

Mara said, "So why don't we switch ourselves off?"

Serena, who'd been humming "Spirit in the Sky" while whittling out the corrosion from her little robot dog, went silent.

Greg said, "We'd have to be damned sure we were going to wake up. I don't want to be stuck in that tank in the dark—drowning—" He got up from his seat and started pacing violently. At least, that was the human mind's translation. Actually, he rose up on his leg stalks and whirled in a floor-polishing circle while his human voice blatted angrily, in the D&D style they'd come to use, "I get up and pace furiously around the room." His hands worked in rapid competence, fixing the repeaters that had blown out in the storm, their skill and the utility of their task making the action the opposite of the agitated fidgeting he clearly wanted to express. He growled, "Look at me! Even when we're off-duty, even when we're upset, it's always some activity to help humanity! And they can't even make sure we have a way back to the ship?"

"I feel you, Greg," Serena said, in the lingo they'd adopted due to the disconnect between their human feelings and robotic exteriors. "But we all knew the risks. They were very clear about that."

Mara laughed. "Yeah, but I trusted them because they're NASA. Come on, no matter what they say, there's nothing they can't do."

Serena smiled. "Nothing *we* can't do, you mean." She raised both her antenna atop the traditional dome of her brainbox. "We astronauts—we always come through! It really is up to us."

I cautioned, "If we wake up on the ship. If we fix whatever's hampering Kyung Mi and make sure everyone's okay. And then we get back to work. When we plug back in—we'll be taking over the Marsbodies again."

Kendra arched a brow. "Isn't that what we want?"

"We'll be overwriting them. Whatever personality they have now."

Kyung Mi's flickering screen cleared. "Whatever personality *we* have," she said clearly.

I felt it then. Holding her fourteen hands and looking into those eyes that had never lied to me, so help me, I felt it.

"We'll disappear—" I gasped.

Kyung Mi's sad smile confirmed it.

Over our private channel, she and I sussed out the situation in a rapid exchange of speculation and data. She'd seen it—for just a moment—our ship.

Mara said frankly, "If we have to remain robots, I'd rather stay on Mars—at least we'd be doing some good—and hey, we'd be on Mars."

Benny took up the chime. "We're aliens here anyway, if you think about it. As robots, we fit right in, 'and hey, we'd be on Mars.'" He pointed a long arm at the ceiling in what had become our "thumbs up" gesture. For once, his silly grin looked entirely appropriate.

But I couldn't let it ride. I just couldn't.

Kyung Mi was up there.

"We have to save them," I said.

They looked at me like I was crazy.

But I knew they understood.

"We have to save *us*," I clarified.

Serena said, with a metallic edge in her voice, "That's not *us* up there any longer."

"It's our mission," Leonard said. His gearbox rattled in his equivalent of a long, frustrated sigh. "If we don't save them, it's a court-martial offense."

"Court-martial?" Sargon scoffed. "They'd court-martial a bunch of robots?"

"No," I said bluntly. "They'd just wipe us clean and start again."

We fell silent then. Outside, the Martian wind raged. I felt a helpless love for this place. Home.

Kyung Mi looked at me, her spindly body graceful, her face on the screen shining serene, like a crowned princess. I loved her so much. I knew she was real. I knew she was herself.

I knew we were happy.

And I knew we couldn't leave her—and the others—alone on that ship, possibly dying, without at least trying to help.

"We can hack into the shipboard computer. Force it to send the sleepers down in their escape pods. We'll collect them and bring them to the oak dome," Mara said decisively. "We can take care of them, and we can still be *us*."

That made so much sense I almost fell for it. "We'd scrub the mission. They haven't been sterilized, they aren't cleared for landing, and they'd have no way of getting back to the ship. We might be destroying their best hope of survival—continued hibernation—without even finding out what's wrong."

Kyung Mi said, "Is there a way to find out?"

"I built a back door to the shipboard computer. It's buried under secret codes, but it's there. I hid it in my personality interface, for emergencies. I'll partition my consciousness, tunnel up, and find out what's really happening. And if I have to—I'll wake my meat self up."

Kyung Mi and I looked at each other. Just as we had all these nights on Mars. That loving gaze. I didn't want to be the lone voice dooming the others. I wanted to save her. Maybe there was a way that only I could go. I—and Kyung Mi, who might be drowning. Whose screen had brightened, resolved, its colors factory sharp. Who might already be dead. Or nearly so. Who might only have moments to live.

Moments that might be enough, if she had help.

I took to the broad channel. Into our shared chat, I poured out my heart. No time for rambling or even data. No time for awkward translations of what a robot feels.

I exerted every bit of memory and creativity I had and called up the scraps of my song.

I wove them together into something new.

Softly, Kyung Mi sang along.

"Do it," Serena said. "Only take us with you, through the shared channel. We can help."

They all voted—two hundred and eighty thumbs up. With the clamor of noisemakers and Bronx cheers. The rattling, enthusiastic fireworks of a robot party.

Our last one.

"Ten," I began, and paused.

"Nine," Kyung Mi answered, with shining eyes.

"Eight!" Kendra shouted.

Together, we counted down.

ABOUT THE AUTHOR

Adele Gardner (none/they/Mx.) is a fiction writer & award-winning poet with work in *Analog* (forthcoming), *Strange Horizons*, *PodCastle*, and *Daily Science Fiction*. A poetry collection, *Halloween Hearts*, is forthcoming from Jackanapes Press. A graduate of the Clarion West Writers Workshop, this genderfluid night owl loves watching samurai films and reading comics with cats. Adele serves as literary executor for father, namesake, and mentor Delbert R. Gardner and guest-edited the Arthuriana issue of *Eye to the Telescope*.

Visitors From Other Stars: The First Interstellar Objects

PAULINE BARMBY

Many SF readers will know Arthur C. Clarke's 1973 novel *Rendezvous with Rama,* in which an alien starship passing through the solar system is at first mistaken for an asteroid. Twenty years after the novel's publication, the first nonfictional interstellar objects were found: interstellar dust grains measured by the Ulysses spacecraft. It took another twenty-five years for the first two bigger-than-a-breadbox interstellar objects to be discovered.

The first, 1I/'Oumuamua (1I means "first interstellar object" while "'Oumuamua" is a Hawai'ian name translated as "scout" or "first to arrive") was elongated like Rama and had other unusual properties that led a few scientists to conjecture that it was an alien spaceship. "Rama" was an early contender for its name. The second interstellar object, 2I/Borisov (named after its discoverer), was clearly a comet and puzzlingly looked nothing like 1I/'Oumuamua. While they're not alien spaceships, these first known visitors from other solar systems are still very exciting to astronomers. They provide an important window into how planets form and planetary systems evolve.

Like comets and asteroids native to our solar system, interstellar objects like 1I/'Oumuamua and 2I/Borisov are difficult to discover because they're small, moving quickly, and relatively rare. 1I/'Oumuamua was discovered when it was already on its way out of the solar system; it was first noticed by astronomer Rob Weryk in images taken with the Pan-STARRS sky survey in October 2017. 2I/Borisov was discovered by Crimean amateur astronomer G. Borisov in August 2019, a few months before its closest approach to the Sun. Compared to 1I/'Oumuamua, 2I/Borisov was easier to detect, being brighter than some solar system comets seen at the same distance from Earth.

Observing the sky positions of 1I/'Oumuamua and 2I/Borisov over multiple nights allowed astronomers to determine the details of their orbits. Everything about the orbits was unusual: both objects were found well away from the plane of the solar system and moving very fast, much faster than the solar system escape speed at their location.

Compared to long-period solar system comets with similar trajectories, the orbits of 1I/'Oumuamua and 2I/Borisov were highly hyperbolic, meaning that these objects were not gravitationally bound to the Sun. Both entered the inner solar system, did hairpin turns, and headed back out of the solar system, their entire visits having lasted only a few months. While 1I/'Oumuamua didn't resemble a typical solar system comet, 2I/Borisov did, developing a tail and coma as it neared the Sun and even undergoing some fragmentation.

Where did 1I/'Oumuamua and 2I/Borisov come from? Most experts think they are likely "planetesimals"—small lumps of rock and ice left over from the formation of their stellar systems and ejected by gravitational interactions, for example with a planet in the system or with a passing nearby star. Even though we know the directions from which both objects entered the solar system, that doesn't tell us their points of origin. Although they were both traveling very fast—far from the gravitational influence of the Sun—their speeds were about twenty-six and thirty-two kilometers per second, or about fifty-nine thousand and seventy-two thousand miles per hour—even at those speeds it takes tens of thousands of years to travel the distance to the nearest stars.

Over that time, the Sun and other stars change position within the Milky Way galaxy, moving in orbits that can be quite complex. To date, astronomers haven't pinpointed definitive origins for either object. 1I/'Oumuamua's speed indicates that it likely came from somewhere within about three thousand lightyears, probably from one of the associations of young stars in our Milky Way neighborhood. One attempt to trace 2I/Borisov's orbit back in time found a close encounter with the nearby red dwarf star Ross 573, about nine hundred and ten thousand years ago. The authors of the paper describing this research are careful to explain that a close encounter doesn't prove Ross 573 was the comet's original host: it could have come from somewhere else and been deflected by the star.

Are there more of these interstellar wanderers? Almost certainly. Some may have already visited our solar system and not been recognized as interstellar, if their orbits weren't measured well enough. Using even the few definitive detections and a knowledge of the efficiency of the detection systems, it's possible to estimate the size of the potential interstellar visitor population. That size is truly enormous: every cubic lightyear of our galaxy contains something like a hundred trillion (1014) objects, which combined have the mass of four Earths.

To get this many objects over the whole galaxy, every star has to be ejecting material to the tune of about ten quadrillion objects each. These are huge numbers but remember that the solar system is very small compared to the galaxy: estimates for the number of interstellar objects in or near the solar system at any given time range from ten to a hundred. Finding them should be made easier by the soon-to-begin Legacy Survey of Space and Time (LSST) project, which will survey the sky from Chile about once a week, using a large telescope able to detect much fainter objects than Pan-STARRS. Estimates are that LSST will detect about one or two interstellar objects per year.

Is the Earth in danger of being hit by these things? A little, but the danger is pretty small compared to homegrown asteroids that are gravitationally bound to the Sun. According to one study, non-interstellar asteroids are about ten thousand times more likely to collide with the Earth than interstellar ones. Solar system asteroids have a range of sizes, with many more small bodies than larger ones, so the more likely collisions are with smaller objects. Assuming interstellar objects have the same range of sizes, this implies that interstellar objects one hundred meters or larger have struck Earth perhaps twenty-five to fifty times in its four-point-six billion year history.

If they're (mostly) not going to hit us, could we visit them instead? It's feasible, but not easy. Since the discovery of 1I/'Oumuamua and 2I/Borisov, many research papers have laid out designs for space missions to visit an interstellar interloper during its brief sojourn near the solar system. Even getting a small spacecraft to an interstellar object would push the limits of current technology, although at least one paper says it's not too late to get to 2I/Borisov if a Jupiter gravity assist is used.

The two big problems are getting a spacecraft to go fast enough to catch an interstellar object, and then slowing down to match the interstellar object's velocity on arrival. (Slowing down isn't absolutely required—for example, the New Horizons mission didn't slow down and go into orbit around Pluto—but a flyby means data can only be gathered for a limited time.) Flybys of the Sun, Jupiter, and Saturn can help with the speedup; electric or magnetic sails could help with the slowdown. It also helps a lot to have enough lead time to launch an intercept mission: 1I/'Oumuamua was detected about a month after its closest approach to the Sun, and 2I/Borisov only a few months before. LSST will help with the issue of lead time: it will improve detection rates enormously, and thus increase the chances that an interstellar visitor will be detected earlier. One study in *The Planetary Science Journal* predicts that visitable objects will be detected about every ten years.

Could we catch a ride on one of these visitors? There's no reason why not, if we could build a spacecraft fast enough to rendezvous with one and the object's surface had properties that would permit attachment. We don't know a lot about how rough or smooth their surfaces might be. Burying your interstellar spacecraft inside an asteroid or comet could help to protect it from impacts with interstellar dust and meteoroids. The downside of hitchhiking is a lack of control over where the hitchhiker goes and a long wait for it to get anywhere.

Although big enough to catch a ride on, 1I/'Oumuamua and 2I/Borisov are so small that they only showed up as points of light in images from even the largest telescopes. To get a clue to their true sizes, astronomers used the same technique used for solar system asteroids and comets. These objects shine by reflected sunlight, so by measuring an object's average brightness, its distances from the Sun and the Earth, and the shininess of its surface (for example, is it covered in dark, rough rock or glittery ice?), astronomers can estimate its size. It's also possible to use brightness variations with time to estimate shape: a tumbling or elongated object will reflect different amounts of light at different times as it presents different faces to the Sun. 2I/Borisov is estimated to be a few hundred meters across, with only tentative brightness variations indicating that it's quite round and rotating very slowly.

On the other hand, observations of 1I/'Oumuamua implied that it was tumbling and nowhere near round or even potato-shaped like many solar system asteroids. Rather, the observations were most consistent with 1I/'Oumuamua being either long and thin—almost needle-shaped—or flat and pancake-shaped. Such shapes are unheard of among solar system asteroids and caused a lot of speculation about the nature of 1I/'Oumuamua.

Analyzing the light from 1I/'Oumuamua and 2I/Borisov with spectrographs allowed astronomers to detect the presence of specific minerals or chemical elements on the objects' surfaces. The spectroscopic observations of 1I/'Oumuamua showed no clear detections of specific molecules, just an overall red color fairly typical of the icy Kuiper Belt objects found in the outskirts of our solar system. Spectroscopy of 2I/Borisov showed molecules like cyanide, diatomic carbon, carbon monoxide, and hydroxide, all commonly found in solar system comets.

When molecules escape from a comet's surface, they can act like tiny rocket thrusters, causing "nongravitational acceleration" and affecting its orbit. 1I/'Oumuamua's orbit indicated that it was undergoing non-gravitational acceleration but puzzlingly, there was no evidence that it underwent the same kind of outgassing as 2I/Borisov. (This could have been because there wasn't time to make the most sensitive observations of 1I/'Oumuamua before it got too far from the Sun.) Besides outgassing, another possible cause of nongravitational acceleration in small solar system objects is radiation pressure from the Sun, the same phenomenon that accelerates light sails. If radiation pressure had caused 1I/'Oumuamua's measured nongravitational acceleration, the object would have to be something much different from a typical asteroid or comet. Calculations showed it would have to be less than a millimeter in thickness and a few thousand kilograms in mass.

Does this mean that 1I/'Oumuamua is an alien spacecraft? Astronomer Abraham (Avi) Loeb coauthored the first paper on the idea of 1I/'Oumuamua as a light sail and recently published a book on the topic: *Extraterrestrial: The First Sign of Intelligent Life Beyond Earth.* In the book he argues that astrobiologists, in their desire to distance themselves from fringe claims about UFOs and alien abductions, are excessively conservative in their willingness to consider anything other than natural explanations for 1I/'Oumuamua's properties.

However, mainstream astronomers have largely dismissed Loeb's claims. While he is a well-known scientist who has held leadership positions in the astronomical community, his expertise is not in planetary science or in observational searches for asteroids and comets. Loeb is also well-known for advocating that scientists should generate many unorthodox ideas because one such idea might be right; many astronomers point out that Loeb doesn't always subject his own wacky ideas to peer review.

Arguments against the interstellar spacecraft hypothesis contend that 1I/'Oumuamua's properties are consistent with it being a natural object. Other configurations than a light sail are consistent with the observations: for example, 1I/'Oumuamua could be a "dust bunny" made up of extremely porous dust grains that are just barely held together, or a nitrogen icicle ejected by the impact of an asteroid or comet on a Pluto-like dwarf planet in another solar system. While the light sail hypothesis could explain 1I/'Oumuamua's elongation and nongravitational acceleration, the orientation that a light sail would need to have is inconsistent with the variations observed in 1I/'Oumuamua's light curve. Other authors have argued that there is no good reason for aliens to send a spacecraft to our solar system. With telescope technology not that much more advanced than ours, they could find out everything about our solar system that a spacecraft visit would tell them, and much more quickly. A flyby visit, such as 1I/'Oumuamua's, doesn't allow much time to gather data in any case.

So where does this leave us? Still with no undisputed interstellar spaceships. While 2I/Borisov seemed to be a reasonably standard comet, the nature of 1I/'Oumuamua is still unsettled, and in particular its unusual shape and rotation are still not well-explained. Both are now too far from Earth to be detected but analysis of the previous observations continues. Now that we know these objects exist, substantial work has gone into planning observations of the next ones so that we can make the most of their limited time in our solar system. The universe has come to us in a fascinating way, and we will be able to use that knowledge to better understand how planets form and change throughout our galaxy.

Further Reading:
- "The Natural History of 'Oumuamua" is a somewhat technical but still accessible summary of what astronomers know (and don't) about this object. https://arxiv.org/pdf/1907.01910.pdf
- "Sending a Spacecraft to Interstellar Comet 2I/Borisov" describes what it would take to reach the comet with current technology. https://arxiv.org/pdf/1909.06348.pdf
- "Research Programs Arising from 'Oumuamua Considered as an Alien Craft" describes interesting research questions that come out of the idea of 1/'Oumuamua as a spaceship; many are still worth investigating even if the hypothesis is disproved. https://arxiv.org/pdf/2111.07895.pdf

ABOUT THE AUTHOR

Pauline Barmby is a Canadian astrophysicist who believes that you can't have too many favorite galaxies. She has been publishing in scientific journals for nearly twenty-five years; her fiction-writing career began in 2022 with work published or forthcoming in *Martian, Tree and Stone,* and Flame Tree Press' *Compelling Science Fiction* anthology. When not reading or writing she runs, knits, and ponders the physics of curling.

A Whole New Wonderful Nightmare: A Conversation with Sam J. Miller

ARLEY SORG

When Sam J. Miller was in preschool, they asked him what he wanted to be when he grew up. He said, "Tyrannosaurus rex."

Miller was born in Hudson, NY, and he escaped when he was eighteen. Trained to be a butcher, the family shop went under; Walmart took over the town. Miller went to Rutgers University, studied cinema studies and Russian language and literature, and perhaps more importantly, met his future husband. He also converted to vegetarianism.

Sam J. Miller's very first published story came out in 1997, in a local anthology called *Out of the Catskills*. From 1997 to 2008 he was getting published steadily, "usually in tiny zines no one ever read or magazines that folded immediately upon publishing my stuff or websites that crashed and burned. Or gay erotica anthologies."

In 2012, Miller attended the Clarion Science Fiction and Fantasy Writers' Workshop. Immediately after, his work began to consistently appear in notable venues. 2013 publications included "The Beasts We Want to Be" in *Electric Velocipede*, "Sabi, Wabi, Aware, Yugen" in *Daily Science Fiction*, and Shirley Jackson Award-winner "57 Reasons for the Slate Quarry Suicides" in *Lightspeed*.

His name continued to land on awards lists. Miller was a Sturgeon and Nebula awards finalist for "We Are the Cloud" (*Lightspeed*, 2014), a World Fantasy Award finalist for "The Heat of Us: Notes Toward an Oral History" (*Uncanny*, 2015), a Shirley Jackson Award nominee for "Angel, Monster, Man" (*Nightmare*, 2016), a Sturgeon, Shirley Jackson, and Nebula Awards finalist for "Things with Beards" (*Clarkesworld*, 2016). Most recently, "Let All the Children Boogie," posted at Tor.com, was a 2021 Nebula finalist. "It's about a bunch of my usual obsessions—queer teenage love and mysterious late night radio broadcasts and maybe time-traveling superintelligences? But mostly it's about David Bowie and Iggy Pop's 'The Passenger,' and the lonesome magic way music can break you out of the bubble of your body."

All four of Sam J. Miller's books landed on the Locus Awards Recommended Reading lists. Debut novel, *The Art of Starving*, came out in 2017 with HarperTeen. Tapping into his own experiences with an eating disorder, he delivered a powerful narrative that resonated with many readers. The book was a Crawford and Lodestar finalist and won an Andre Norton Award. *Blackfish City* was published by HarperCollins imprint Ecco in 2018, earning a Nebula Award nomination and winning a John W. Campbell Memorial Award.

Miller brought his love of dinosaurs into novel *Destroy All Monsters*, published by HarperTeen in 2019 to positive reviews. In his 2020 novel *The Blade Between*, published by Ecco, he revisited his childhood home of Hudson. "It's a great microcosm for America as a whole because it's full of good people who do bad things, and vice versa, and all the racism and homophobia and toxic masculinity that are so essential to understanding the fucked-up American moment we currently find ourselves in are on full display in Hudson."

Miller is known as an outspoken activist and community organizer. "When I'm not trying to smash the system via somewhat-subversive stories, I'm trying to smash the system by organizing poor people to fight collectively for social justice. I spent fifteen years as a community organizer at Picture the Homeless, where I played a part in organizing billions of amazing protests and events, helped win over one hundred and twenty policy and legislative victories, and I coordinated the writing of a major report that was required reading in urban planning courses at Columbia University—and was banned in New York State prisons."

Sam J. Miller's debut collection is *Boys, Beasts & Men*, just out (June, 2022) from Tachyon Publications.

What were the books, stories, or authors that were important to you when you first started getting into genre fiction, and do you see their influence in the things that you write?

I think of Ray Bradbury and Octavia Butler as my science fiction mom and dad, they're the ones who got me most excited about the possibilities of the genre, and the ones that I see on the page the most to this day. Bradbury showed me all the ways the world can be wonderful and gave me that sense of excitement and poetry that I still try to carry forward. And Octavia Butler showed me all the ways the world can be terrible, and the ways that people can fight back, and how science fiction can be a form of activism.

You've been writing and publishing since roughly 2003, but you really hit the scene in 2013. You've been publishing short fiction consistently since then. You've also been publishing books consistently since your 2017 debut, *The Art of Starving*. You've had a book come out every year except for 2021. What does it take to stay in the game and to sustain a career?

Listen, I'm not saying you have to have a bottomless hole of insecurity and loneliness and an undying thirst for attention and external validation to make it as a writer, but in my case, it sure did help! I think above all you have to really love the act of fiction, as a reader and as a writer, and you have to be committed to doing it no matter what happens. That includes rejection, failure, difficulty . . . but it also includes the ups as well as the downs. You might have a great year—or two—or five—but everything ebbs and flows, and you're never *done,* you never feel like, *Okay, I'm good, I've achieved everything I need to achieve, and I can take a break.* At least, I don't.

Are there important differences in the way you approach writing novels compared to the way you approach shorter work?

No, they both tend to spring up like mystery seeds that got planted in the soil of my brain . . . and I'll spend a day or a week or a decade tending to it, watering it, watching it wither, watching it thrive, forgetting about it, obsessing over it, before I can figure out what it will be. The orcamancer from *Blackfish City* showed up one day in my head, and I spent a long time thinking she wanted to be a short story, before it was clear to me her story was so big it needed a novel.

For me, your work usually combines intriguing characters who are grounded—who feel real—with interesting ideas, plus a compelling problem. It's a lot to manage, but you pull it off seamlessly, delivering consistently great fiction. What is the key to effectively pulling all these elements together?

Awwww, thank you so much for saying so! Ultimately, I like a challenge. I love to set myself ambitious goals for weird big complicated little stories that try to do a lot. Sometimes I think I am successful, and I pulled it all off. Sometimes I think I was . . . less so. But that's a subjective perspective, and there have definitely been stories of mine that I personally felt were less strong—but got a great response—and others that I was more proud of and didn't get much attention—so at the end of the day we're all just readers, with blind spots and biases and triggers, so I take comfort in the total absence of objective standards of artistic merit.

Right out the gate you won a Shirley Jackson Award for "57 Reasons for the Slate Quarry Suicides," and you've been on awards ballots and mentions ever since. Do awards and acclaim have an impact on your writing or process?

I wish I was strong enough to not need them, or to say, "awards don't matter," but . . . yeah, it goes back to the bottomless hole of insecurity and self-doubt and need for external validation, lol. Writing can feel so lonely. Any form of recognition just reminds me that someone somewhere connected with my work, and that's so rare and special.

What was "breaking in" like for you, and how did it happen? At what point did you feel like you had broken in?

"Breaking in" is actually a very apt euphemism here, because it truly did feel like intruding upon a space that wasn't necessarily meant for me. Even though I had always loved the work of queer speculative authors like Samuel Delany and Tom Disch, I didn't see a ton of queer stuff getting published and celebrated, and I definitely spent a long time shopping around queer SFF novels nobody wanted. There were so many milestones along the way, however, and every tiny zine publication or rejection-with-comments from a major outlet felt important and transformative. Honestly, I'd say it wasn't until I won the Nebula Award for *The Art of Starving* that I felt like I could chill a tiny bit. But that only lasted a week or so.

Your debut collection, Boys, Beasts & Men, goes all the way back to 2013 publications, such as "The Beasts We Want to Be" and "57 Reasons for the Slate Quarry Suicides," but also offers newer pieces such as "Sun in an Empty Room." Looking at this spectrum of work over the course of a decade, do you see specific ways in which your writing has changed?

My prime directive when it comes to writing short fiction is never to repeat myself, which means that over the twenty-five years since I first published a short story in a raggedy little local anthology, I have tried to set myself increasingly challenging goals, and push myself to attempt new and difficult things with my stories. So, there is definitely a bedrock of Me that's resonant throughout these stories, but there's also a shifting evolution in terms of what I can accomplish with tone and theme and framework and formal conceit and just generally trying to constantly make better use of the awesome tool kit that speculative fiction gives us all.

The collection features fourteen stories, which is just under half of the short fiction you have out. How were stories selected? Is there an organizational principle at work—is it a "best of" or do selections follow a theme?

The organizing principle in *Boys, Beasts & Men* is the age of the protagonist, going from the eight-year-old boy who narrates "Allosaurus Burgers" (the first story in the book) to the antique couch who narrates "Sun in an Empty Room" (the last). I definitely tried to include as many stories that seemed to resonate with readers as possible, but I also wanted to tell a unified story about how the world makes us monsters, so I omitted many stories that seemed less directly connected to that core theme.

What can you tell us about "Sun in an Empty Room"—without "spoiling" the read too much?

It's my white whale, the thing I spent years and years trying to land. I wrote it in 2008, and it was rejected by ninety-nine literary and speculative journals. And it's how I met the awesome Fran Wilde. I submitted it to *Apex* when she was a slush reader there, and she tried her best to get it published, but then-editor-in-chief Lynne M. Thomas wasn't feeling it. But Fran sent me a super encouraging note (this was before I made my first pro sale and was really struggling, so encouraging words went a looooong way!), and we're buddies to this day.

Lynne went on to cofound *Uncanny Magazine* and published my story "The Heat Of Us" (also included in *Boys, Beasts & Men*), and we're buddies too, so . . . keep on going, even when it sucks, the pain of rejection can make you better, and sometimes the people who tell you *No* now will one day be your friends.

If readers looked at three stories in this book, what would you want them to be, and why?

Well, when I got the ARC I reread "Shucked" for the first time since submitting it to *F&SF*, and I was . . . kinda impressed? Whoever I was when I wrote it, he was pretty great. And I think "Things With Beards" might be the most *me* story I've written. Finally, there's a framing story that incorporates every story in the book into one cohesive narrative (hopefully), and that's made up of short vignettes before and after every story, and I think it's pretty cool.

Which, for you, were the stories that were most challenging to write? What made them challenging, and how did you face those challenges?

Each story is a whole new wonderful nightmare. I can't say that any of them were particularly easy to write, but, also, I enjoy the process so much that I'm hard-pressed to say they were *difficult*. Like it's like playing a really hard really great video game—even when it's kicking your ass, it's still a ton of fun.

Looking at your career so far, are there themes and ideas in your fiction that you often come back to, that stand out as more important to you, or about which you feel passionate?

My work is always about how humans are amazing, and how they are terrible. How much great cool stuff we do, and how much atrocity. And how even really awesome people do really shitty things. These stories look at that through the lens of patriarchy, toxic masculinity, queerness, and complicity and resistance, which just never gets boring to me lol.

Is there anything else you'd like readers to know about this book?

That the incredible Amal El-Mohtar wrote the introduction! And it's amazing! Seriously made me choke up when I read it. In 2014, when my short story "We Are the Cloud" (included in the collection) was published in *Lightspeed*, it got some super homophobic reviews, which suuuuuuuuuucked—any LGBTQIA+ SFF writer can tell you that queering the genre means coming up against a whole lot of really vicious trolls—and Amal wrote the most beautiful review/defense of the story; that's how I knew she'd be the perfect person to do the introduction.

Are there stories over the course of your career that you were especially happy with, that you felt very strongly about, but that, for whatever reasons, just didn't get noticed the way other pieces did?

TONS!! It's a constant source of puzzlement, what hits and what doesn't. What factors go into that. But then again, you never know—life is long, and things have a way of coming and going, including stories. I thought my Tor.com story "The Future of Hunger in the Age of Programmable Matter" kinda sank like a stone, but then it got included in a Japanese anthology of the world's best science fiction shorts from the 2010s, so . . . you never know. And you gotta just keep going.

What else are you working on now, and what do you have coming up that you can tell us about?

My pandemic project was to teach myself programming so I could make a video game. That's coming along nicely—it's a very queer RPG. And I am hard at work on a new novel. And short stories. All the things, really.

ABOUT THE AUTHOR

Arley Sorg is co-Editor-in-Chief at *Fantasy Magazine* and a 2021 World Fantasy Award Finalist. He is also a finalist for two 2022 Ignyte Awards, for his work as a critic as well as for his creative nonfiction. Arley is senior editor at *Locus Magazine*, associate editor at both *Lightspeed* & *Nightmare*, and a columnist for *The Magazine of Fantasy and Science Fiction*. He takes on multiple roles, including slush reader, movie reviewer, and book reviewer, and conducts interviews for multiple venues, including *Clarkesworld Magazine* and his own site: arleysorg.com. He has taught classes and run workshops for Clarion West, *Augur Magazine*, and more, and has been a guest speaker at a range of events. Arley grew up in England, Hawaii, and Colorado, and studied Asian Religions at Pitzer College. He lives in the SF Bay Area and writes in local coffee shops when he can. Arley is a 2014 Odyssey Writing Workshop graduate.

Everyday Dystopia:
A Conversation with Samit Basu
ARLEY SORG

Samit Basu was born and raised in Kolkata in West Bengal, India. He earned a degree in economics at Presidency College and completed a course in broadcasting and documentary filmmaking at the University of Westminster in London.

Basu's debut novel, *The Simoqin Prophecies*, "India's first ever SFF (science fiction/fantasy) genre novel in English," was published by Penguin India in 2004. Marketed as "Monty Python meets the Ramayana," among other things, it was an immediate national bestseller in India, and ultimately garnered praise at venues such as *The Telegraph* and *Locus*. Book two in the GameWorld trilogy, *The Manticore's Secret*, came out in 2005 and book three, *The Unwaba Revelations*, followed in 2007.

In 2007, Basu also wrote notable graphic stories with Virgin Comics (now Liquid Comics), including the *Devi* series beginning with #3:

Namaha, and *The Tall Tales of Vishnu Sharma: Panchatantra*. 2010 brought Basu's collaboration with Mike Carey, a comic book called *Untouchable*, published by Dynamite and Liquid; and in 2011 he began comic book series *Unholi* with Graphic India. In 2013 he published *Local Monsters* with Westland. Along the way, he occasionally dabbled in short fiction such as "Alienation" in 2005 anthology *The HarperCollins Book of New Indian Fiction*, "Rocket Kumar" in 2008 Scholastic India anthology *Superhero*, "Electric Sonalika" in 2012 anthology *The Apex Book of World SF 2*, and a handful more.

Not to be slowed down by these projects, Basu also published a YA historical novel called *Terror on the Titanic* with Scholastic India in 2009. Then in 2012, Titan published superhero novel *Turbulence*. Sequel *Resistance* came in 2014, along with the first in his series of children's books, *The Adventures of Stoob: Testing Times* (with Rupa imprint Red Turtle). Samit Basu wrote and codirected the film *House Arrest*, released on Netflix in 2019.

A year later, novel *Chosen Spirits* was published by Simon and Schuster India. It received a slew of rave reviews in India as well as the US, including coverage at respected science fiction venues such as *Strange Horizons* and *Locus*. *Chosen Spirits* landed on the Locus Recommended Reading list and was a finalist for the JCB Prize for literature. *The City Inside* is the highly anticipated US release of *Chosen Spirits*, due from Tordotcom publishing on June 7, 2022.

"I live across three cities, including a Mumbai flat on an island famous for smuggling, featuring tall buildings where local celebrities hide their second families to avoid the media. In Delhi, I have had my house invaded by monkeys five times over the years: my deal with them now is I will put them in books and screenplays, and they will leave me alone."

What were the first SFF books or stories that were important to you, and do you feel like they have influenced your writing in any important ways?

I grew up with no understanding of genre, because that's not how Indian bookstores worked, so I just read everything, not knowing that stories had borders. I remember being absolutely mesmerized by *The Hobbit/ LOTR* as a preteen, and I think I read Asimov in middle school. *Hitchhiker's Guide* was also an early love, and then when I was a bit older the biggest influence was Discworld, which I devoured, and which was definitely one of the underlying pillars of my first novel, *The Simoqin*

Prophecies. The others were various fantastical early influences: an obsession with world myth, fables from everywhere, children's stories, and fantasy films in Bengali. And genre films and shows that were global blockbusters, plus eighties and nineties animation, and comics wherever I could get them, starting with Asterix and Tintin.

My understanding of genre as a wing of publishing only began after my first novel was published: until then I'd only thought of fantasy and SF as useful descriptors of story, not as closed gates with their own conformities. I'm influenced by everything I read and see, and I'm not sure what my biggest influences are now: whatever they are, they're current work.

How did you get into writing seriously, and what was your journey to "breaking in"?

It was fairly dramatic. I think I'd always wanted to be a writer, or do something in a creative field, but that really wasn't something someone from my generation and demographic did in India. It's still not something that's a career, at least for people who have to think about earning money, unless they're sufficiently socially privileged, very lucky, and very stubborn, and I've been all three. So, I did all the things I was supposed to do as a student, and at twenty-one, I found myself joining India's top MBA school with absolutely no urge to be there. I'd promised myself I would drop whatever I was doing in life and write a novel the moment I had an idea I was sure could be a book.

This happened a few weeks into the first term, and to my absolute surprise, when I told my closest family and friends about it, that I really wanted to give the book a shot, they all said I should! Emboldened by these reckless people and their mix of confidence in me and possibly exhaustion at my moaning, I went back home, wrote a novel, and I think around a couple of years later it was published by Penguin in India. I cannot begin to tell you how ignorant I was about publishing, a life in the arts, anything. It wasn't just that I was young, it was really a different era, pre-social media, pre-Gmail, even, and there was just no information publicly available.

The book did really well though: lots of lovely reviews, bestseller lists for many months. No major Indian (English) publisher had published/marketed SFF before, and Penguin didn't try to smuggle me in under the magic realism/mythological respectability blankets. I was twenty-three at the time, and it was a time when India had globalist/progressive goals, so I got a lot of attention. That was eighteen years ago, and I've been writing for a living ever since across books, comics, film/TV, and nonfiction in a wide range of genres.

Breaking into the UK and the US happened in 2012/13 with *Turbulence*, a superhero novel, from Titan. Big four break-in happened, well, now. The decade in the middle has mostly been spent in Bollywood meetings and development hells.

The City Inside may get the attention of many new readers, but you've actually been writing and publishing for roughly twenty years. Has your writing changed in specific ways since The Simoqin Prophecies came out in 2003?

My writing's changed continuously, mostly because I've been traveling across genres and media a lot, partly to be able to keep writing for a living and partly because I really like a wide range of genres and media (though if I had to pick one of each, it would be speculative fiction novels), and hopefully I'm also growing as a writer with age and exposure and experience.

Non-writing creative work like direction or film/comics editing changes your writing as well. It's difficult to articulate the specifics or figure out what comes from where, especially over two decades. I think you learn a lot from code-switching in both life and work. Each genre, each medium teaches you different things, each has its challenges and its conformities. So, figuring out how to retain your own identity and develop your own voice is consistently interesting and always challenging. Also, choosing projects is just as important as executing them as well you can: I've hopefully gotten better at both.

The City Inside has a number of fun innovations, such as the screen-shirt. What are a few of your favorites?

When I decided to set *The City Inside* approximately a decade in the future, I set myself a constraint: I would use tech that had already been invented in some form at least as a prototype, make only slight extensions to it that would be very feasible to imagine a decade in the future, and focus really on how it would be used, because the same tech is used very differently in India than it is in the West, not just in different regions but also different communities and privilege levels. Essentially keeping the focus on the social and political use and impact of the tech more than the tech itself.

So my favorite innovations are the Flow, the viewer-personalized future-influencer livestream-social media-reality TV-gaming-news hybrid that the protagonists produce and manage at work; Tavata, the smart-tattoo upgrade for culture-customizable consent-matching/ dating/spouse-arranging/sex-policing; the various methods used by shadowy resistance groups for protest and action from spray-paint drones to virtual dens; and of course Narad the digital assistant, named after the messenger/gossipmonger/spy of Hindu myth.

There are some sharp, somewhat cynical observations on sociopolitical activism in the narrative. I'm reminded of the way that many activists from famous eras in the US later became businesspeople, or otherwise affluent participants in the systems they had stood against. Are you taking a position through your fiction, or is this more about just imagining and fictionalizing future possibilities?

Somewhere in between, because the inspiration for these moments of cynicism comes from the behavior of present-day influencers I know, and many present-day politicians who have conveniently shown people much hope and then switched camps as the country slides further into a pit. Looking into the future, I could only imagine that the next generation of people like them would be under even more pressure and trusting any public figure to have fixed values and positions would be even more dangerous—all of this to make the journey of the protagonists toward figuring out their own forms of resolve and resistance more difficult.

One of the things that struck me about Joey's character was her role as family mediator, and to some extent, family caretaker in general. What were your inspirations for this character, and what were your favorite things about writing her?

All the people in *The City Inside* are inspired by or shameless chimaeras of people I know or have met in real life, between close friends and family and memorable single meetings. Joey is a few of my favorite people in the real world, and there's a lot of my feelings in there as well. But her top five immediate sources are all women I know, who are in a particular range of professions—editors, team leaders, producers—and all have to handle a tremendous amount of responsibility and stress. They had certain similarities: all immensely capable, underappreciated, overcommitted, non-narcissistic, often under-rewarded, empathetic, reluctantly authority-exerting, under-radar system-changing, often gaslit, often permanently found cleaning up after emotionally under-developed charismatic sociopaths. And all very angry about the state of the world and guilty about not doing enough to improve it even if they were doing a lot. So, Joey was great fun to write: I knew her very well.

What was the initial inspiration for this book, and how did it develop?

I wanted to write a near-future story set in the city I live in, which is Delhi, the political, media, and cultural capital of India. A lot of this desire came out of anger at the present and anxiety about the future. I also spend a lot of time on the Internet, and it began to become really obvious that people all over the world were facing the same crises and were frustrated about the same lack of response, even if everyone was looking at their local chaos-pit.

My initial plan was to map out the first half of this century for South Asia, using current and speculative nonfiction, the news both real and propaganda, and people and places I broadly knew. The central characters would be from the generation in their teens now, people born into a world changing too fast for most present-day adults to understand. The book itself I'd visualized as part tech-dystopia, part cyberpunk, three sections each a decade apart. I wanted to track my protagonists as they escaped or defeated the multiple-choice apocalypses currently threatening our world, with an extra layer of India-specific chaos.

I ended up, a few years of research later, doing something quite different. And I think it was because I actually lived in the middle of the world I was trying to make a near-future fictional extension of, and it's not a dystopia, or cyberpunk, if you live inside a world: it's just everyday life.

The City Inside was originally published in India as Chosen Spirits. Did you make any notable changes for its US incarnation?

I made some additions to the world of the novel, mostly to factor in the events of 2020 and as much of 2021 as I could in the decade-ago backstory. I know it's not the job of science fiction to accurately predict the future, but a lot of the worldbuilding was based on the news, long-form and speculative nonfiction in various media, and even in its earliest drafts I was making adjustments constantly because bad things

132

I'd thought were five years away were happening on a weekly basis. The first two pandemic waves were simply too impactful to leave out of any reality-adjacent worldbuild, I thought. Apart from that, a few structural adjustments suggested by my Tordotcom editors, Sanaa Ali-Virani and Ruoxi Chen, who were an absolute delight to work with.

What were some of your biggest challenges in writing this book, and how did you deal with those challenges?

I ended up making a novel out of just the planned first section of the three I described earlier because the more I immersed myself in research and early drafts the clearer it became that there was no tech-led world-saving possible here, and no revolution that could guarantee sustainable social progress and the defeat of evils millennia old. That the answer lay not in action set pieces or the defeat of a specific set of villains, but in multigenerational, multi-community, excruciatingly slow progress, and it would be vaguely exploitative to suggest otherwise in a book very closely overlaid on the real world. So, I started focusing more on the protagonists coping with and learning from their surroundings, finding the courage to stop looking away from their very dangerous world, and making their journeys toward becoming the people they needed to be to save whatever their own worlds were.

What for you is the heart of the story for The City Inside? What is important for people to know about this book?

The City Inside is about two people coming to terms with a very harsh world and finding their own ways into action. In a world that wants to measure, manipulate, and dominate them, they must find out who they really are in the middle of endless lies and distraction, what they really want in a shape-shifting, cloudy, reality-set, and how to make the world around them better to the extent of their abilities.

What should people know? It's a near-future anti-dystopian science fiction novel set in Delhi about a decade from now. Heat waves, water shortage, incredible inequality, surveillance capitalism, culture clashes, dysfunctional families/friendships/work spaces/urban societies.

Our protagonist Joey is a Reality Controller, who manages a Flowstar, an influencer/celebrity who is also her college ex. She oversees and optimizes his multimedia multi-reality livestreams with great success and manages her own life as best as she can, keeping in mind her own safety, and her family's. But one day she impulsively offers a job to a childhood friend, Rudra, a recluse estranged from his powerful and very shady family. They offend people they shouldn't in the process, and their lives spin out of control.

You have some short fiction out. Are you more comfortable writing longer works?

I'm much more comfortable with longer work, mostly because when I have an idea I really like, I enjoy living in it for as long as I can. Most of the short story ideas I have go into a folder, and then get absorbed into novels.

What else are you working on, what do you have coming up that you'd like people to know about?

Another novel, hopefully next year, and I'm waiting for Tordotcom to announce it! It has several themes in common with *The City Inside*, and has all the action set pieces, plot twists, romance, and shenanigans that I had to hold myself back from in an attempt to foreground the interiority of *TCI*. Also, some film things I'm working on, but those aren't real until they're on screen. I know what the next few books I want to write are and definitely want to direct more in the TV/film space as well.

ABOUT THE AUTHOR

Arley Sorg is co-Editor-in-Chief at *Fantasy Magazine* and a 2021 World Fantasy Award Finalist. He is also a finalist for two 2022 Ignyte Awards, for his work as a critic as well as for his creative nonfiction. Arley is senior editor at *Locus Magazine*, associate editor at both *Lightspeed* & *Nightmare*, and a columnist for *The Magazine of Fantasy and Science Fiction*. He takes on multiple roles, including slush reader, movie reviewer, and book reviewer, and conducts interviews for multiple venues, including *Clarkesworld Magazine* and his own site: arleysorg.com. He has taught classes and run workshops for Clarion West, *Augur Magazine*, and more, and has been a guest speaker at a range of events. Arley grew up in England, Hawaii, and Colorado, and studied Asian Religions at Pitzer College. He lives in the SF Bay Area and writes in local coffee shops when he can. Arley is a 2014 Odyssey Writing Workshop graduate.

Editor's Desk:
Managing This Expectation
NEIL CLARKE

I've made no secret that I find writing these editorials to be difficult. It's primarily because I'm a very slow writer, but also because it often feels like I'm standing in an empty field talking to myself. What other jobs have this sort of thing as an expectation? Is this the SF equivalent of a post-game locker room press conference? I know some editors who appear to follow that path, talking about the different players/authors and their actions/stories in this month's game/issue. Trying to do that would just make my head spin. Maybe there's something else . . .

How about the post-launch mission briefing where I tell you how the team is doing and what we hope to see in the days ahead? I've done some of those and this month I could even give you a brief on how fictionauts R.S.A. Garcia, Ray Nayler, and Suzanne Palmer have been selected as finalists for the eagerly-awaited 2022 Sturgeon Award mission, or how Samantha Murray just successfully landed a winning best novella at the 2021 Aurealis Awards in May.

Or perhaps, I'm filing a report of "criminal" acts? Earlier this week I was the victim of an ageist attack suggesting that I was "too old to be editing one of the leading science fiction magazines" and I should "get out of the way" so someone younger can do it. I'm only fifty-five, not the oldest editor I know, and not about to give up the magazine I started over one person's disrespectful opinion on the matter. Their punishment is measured by the amount of time I continue to edit *Clarkesworld*.

Could be that it's like being a referee, outlining how we'd like to see the game played? It's perfectly fair to criticize or celebrate the finalists or winners of any award. Science fiction is a broad field with a variety of styles that might not appeal to everyone and the awards will reflect some of that. It's only natural to be thrilled or disappointed when your favorite player wins, loses, or is benched. That said, we want a fair fight here. There should be no punching below the belt–criticizing or campaigning against based on anything other than the work they've done.

How about a school paper about my family vacation? It was several days of heavy fog and rain at the shore. We visited our old hotel and discovered that it had already been bulldozed to make room for four four-million-dollar condos on the boardwalk. Despite the weather, a good time was had by all. It ended too soon and I can't wait to go back, hopefully sometime I can actually see the sky and the ocean.

I'll have to keep thinking about this. There must be some path that will make this feel more natural. Maybe I should look into having an AI write these editorials . . . or just bring in someone younger with all the answers. (Too soon?) I think I'll just continue to wander around this field until I figure it out.

ABOUT THE AUTHOR

Neil Clarke is the editor of *Clarkesworld Magazine* and *Forever Magazine*; owner of Wyrm Publishing; and a ten-time Hugo Award Nominee for Best Editor (short form). His anthologies include *Upgraded, Galactic Empires, More Human Than Human, Touchable Unreality, The Final Frontier, Not One of Us, The Eagle has Landed,* and the Best Science Fiction of the Years series. His latest anthology, *The Best Science Fiction of the Year: Volume 6,* is now available from Night Shade Books. He currently lives in NJ with his wife and two sons.

The Pod

COVER ART BY EDDIE MENDOZA

Eddie Mendoza is a concept artist based in San Francisco. He primarily works in the video game industry and has contributed to titles such as Epic Game's Paragon, Unreal Tournament, Star Wars Armada, and Warhammer 40K. He has also worked for a wide variety of clients some of which include Warner Bros, EA DICE, Unity VR, and Scribble Pad Studios. His passion for all things architectural and robotic inspires his work and he enjoys dreaming of both dystopian and utopian visions of the future. In his free time, he enjoys world-building and crafting his own video games—the latest of which is "Hunted"—a first person shooter where humans are pitted against dinosaurs on reality TV.

CPSIA information can be obtained
at www.ICGtesting.com
Printed in the USA
JSHW021501140622
26966JS00004B/27